PUFFIN BOOKS

Editor: *Kaye Webb*

The Ten Tales of Shellover

When Shellover first appeared in Mrs Candy's garden the Cow couldn't eat, the Seven Black Hens were restless, the Dog dug up an old bone, and the Cat couldn't even be bothered to look at the Sparrows. And the worst of it was Mrs Candy *liked* him. But when they found he had travelled the world and could Tell Stories everything was all right again.

There were ten stories, one for each of them, and each better than the last, and all of them just right for reading at bedtime or any other time. Each one is as complete and satisfying as Shellover's breakfasts on Mrs Candy's lettuces.

Illustrated by Antony Maitland

THE TEN
TALES OF
SHELLOVER

Ruth Ainsworth

Penguin Books

Penguin Books Ltd, Harmondsworth, Middlesex, England
Penguin Books Australia Ltd, Ringwood, Victoria, Australia

—

First published by André Deutsch 1963
Published in Puffin Books 1967
Reprinted 1970, 1971
Copyright © Ruth Ainsworth, 1963

—

Made and printed in Great Britain by
Hazell Watson & Viney Ltd,
Aylesbury, Bucks
Set in Linotype Pilgrim

This book is sold subject to the condition
that it shall not, by way of trade or otherwise,
be lent, re-sold, hired out, or otherwise circulated
without the publisher's prior consent in any form of
binding or cover other than that in which it is
published and without a similar condition
including this condition being imposed
on the subsequent purchaser

Contents

A Stranger in the Garden

ONE morning, the sun was shining in the windows of Mrs Candy's cottage and the birds were singing in her apple tree. Everything looked the same as usual except the chimney. There was no smoke coming out of it.

Mrs Candy's pets knew there was something different. They knew there was something wrong. They had lost the nice, safe, comfortable feeling they always had when they woke up and began another day.

The Cow could not settle to her breakfast of fresh green grass because she knew it was time to be milked. She waited for the chink of the milking pail and for Mrs Candy's cheerful, 'Good morning, my dear.' Surely Mrs Candy had not forgotten her? Such a thing had never happened before.

The seven black Hens were restless too. They sat on their perch in the hen-house, pushing each other and fluffing out their feathers. There was a little window in the hen-house: they could look through and they saw the sparrows having a bath in their drinking water. This made them very cross indeed. Why ever didn't Mrs Candy come and unlatch the door and let them out? They would drive those bad-mannered sparrows away in a jiffy.

The Dog dug up an old bone from under a bush just for something to do to pass the time. He felt restless, too. Every morning he carried sticks in his mouth and laid them in the hearth to help Mrs Candy when she lit the fire. But this morning she had not even raked out the ashes. What was wrong?

7

As for the Cat, he sat on the window-sill and blinked. He took no notice of the sparrows having their bath. He took no notice of anyone or anything. He just dreamed of the moment when Mrs Candy poured milk into his saucer, and added a little hot water to please him, and set the saucer on the hearth-rug.

'This is too bad!' said the Cat at last, licking his dry lips with his rough pink tongue. 'No fire! No breakfast! No cheerful word! Let's call Mrs Candy. She always comes when we call her.'

'Yes, let's,' agreed the others. 'Let's call loudly.'

> 'Moo – moo – moo!
> Milk me do!'

mooed the Cow.

> 'Let us out! Let us out!
> Let us scratch round about!'

clucked the Hens.

> 'What, no cinders? No sticks?
> We shall be in a fix!'

barked the Dog.

> 'Make the fire! Make the tea!
> Pour my milk out for me!'

mewed the Cat.

To their surprise, there was no sound of hurrying feet and no Mrs Candy flying here, there, and everywhere, trying to attend to all her family at once.

'We must find out what has gone wrong,' said the Cow, pushing open the gate which led from the field to the yard. The Hens pressed against their little window to get a good view of what was going on. The Cat and the Dog followed

8

the Cow, the Cat waving his tail and the Dog sniffing along the ground to find out if any strangers had been near.

They found Mrs Candy in the garden, kneeling on the grass behind the apple tree, holding something in her hands and looking at it as if it were very dear and wonderful. But it did not look wonderful to them. It just looked dark and solid and dull.

'Please drop that stone and milk me,' begged the Cow.

'Throw that old log on the fire and light it,' said the Dog.

'I'm more important than that lump of rock,' pleaded the Cat. 'Please get me my breakfast.'

'Oh dear!' said Mrs Candy, looking at her family. 'I forgot all about you. I was pulling up a weed from among the pansies, when I saw this strange and interesting thing on the ground. It isn't just wood or stone. It is ALIVE. I heard it snore. I was trying to make it wake up and come out and show itself when you all came along. Well, I must try again later on.'

She laid the strange thing very tenderly on a patch of grass and began to rub bits of soil off its back with the corner of her apron.

'I'll be back again soon,' she whispered to it, though there was no ear visible for it to hear with.

The pets felt upset. They did not like what they had seen and heard. Till then, Mrs Candy had only wanted them for her children. Now she seemed to want this strange thing as well. It wasn't fair.

The Hens ate their corn without spreading their wings for Mrs Candy to stroke them. The Cat did not purr and the Dog never wagged his tail. The Cow did not lean her head on Mrs Candy's shoulder when she had been milked. But Mrs Candy did not appear to mind. She drank one cup of tea instead of three and piled up the dirty plates and went back to the apple tree. The pets heard her give a cry of joy and call out:

'Come and look! Come and see for yourselves!'

'I shan't bother to go,' growled the Dog, and the others agreed that they would not go either. But really they were longing to know what had happened.

After a time the Cat said:

'We might just take a walk in the sun and see if any new pansies have opened.'

'We'll come too. There are fine fat worms among the pansies,' said the Hens.

'Then I'll come to take care of you,' said the Dog.

The Cow did not make any remark as she was busy chewing, but she followed the others.

Mrs Candy was smiling with joy, and the strange thing, which had looked both dead and dull, had put out a flat little head at one end, a short pointed tail at the other, and four stumpy legs at the sides.

'Tell me who you are,' begged Mrs Candy. 'Tell me your name and where you come from.'

'I hope it speaks a language no one understands,' muttered the Cat. But he hoped in vain. The strange thing spoke perfect English.

'My name is Shellover the Tortoise and I come from far away over the sea. I should like to walk about in this garden and perhaps live here always if it pleases me.'

('Always!' repeated the animals. 'How terrible!')

'Walk anywhere you like,' said Mrs Candy.

Shellover the Tortoise set off as briskly as he could and marched across the parsley bed. The pets all looked up at Mrs Candy. Surely she would tell him to be careful! Surely she would scold him for crushing the young parsley! But no, she never said a word.

Then he pushed his way through the carrots and among the beans till he came to the lettuces. The lettuce bed was Mrs Candy's great pride. Not a Hen dared scratch anywhere near it and the animals took care never to set foot in it. But Tortoise had no such fears. He walked boldly up to the first lettuce and took a large bite and said:

'Not bad!'

Then he went to the next lettuce and took another bite and said:

'I've tasted worse!'

Then he tried the third and said:

'Not much heart but a good flavour!'

The pets expected Mrs Candy to blow up with rage, but she only remarked that a few sunny days would work wonders. The hearts would improve.

'I shall have a nap now,' said Shellover the Tortoise, tucking his head and tail and legs out of sight. Gentle breathing showed that he was asleep at once.

'I do hope he settles here,' said Mrs Candy, going into the cottage to get on with her work. 'It will be so nice to have another new animal in the family, so different from the others.'

'What a horrid day it has been,' said the Cat, when she had gone. 'Breakfast late and Mrs Candy not loving us any more and this dreadful Tortoise thing come to live here.'

'And the day isn't over yet,' added the Dog. 'It is only the morning. However shall we get through the afternoon and evening?'

'Then there's tomorrow,' clucked the Hens.

'And the day after that.'

'And the day after the day after that.'

'We can't bear it,' said the Cow. 'We were so happy just by ourselves. We must do something about it. We must get rid of this Tortoise fellow.'

'But how can we get rid of him?' asked the others.

'We could throw him in the pond,' said the Cat, who hated water. 'But perhaps he can swim.'

'I could toss him over the hedge into the lane,' said the Cow, 'but he might find his way back and tell tales to Mrs Candy.'

'We'll bury him,' said the Dog. 'I'll dig a deep, dark hole. We'll lay him in very gently so as not to wake him, and he'll never know he has been buried.'

The Dog began to dig a hole with his paws and the others helped. When the hole was deep and dark, they laid Shellover the Tortoise gently at the bottom and covered him over. He never moved or made a sound.

The pets crept away and tried to forget the hole and what was in it. But they couldn't quite forget. They all had a horrid morning, wondering if Tortoise had waked up and wondering what Mrs Candy would say if she found out what they had done.

When dinner time came, Mrs Candy clapped her hands to let them know it was time to come in, but they didn't feel hungry. They walked slowly to the cottage door, hanging their heads. The Cat even wiped his eyes with the tip of his tail.

On the doorstep, smiling and chuckling, was Shellover the Tortoise.

'Do you see what I see?' gasped the Dog.

'Yes we do,' said the others. 'We do indeed.'

Tortoise was laughing so much he could hardly speak.

'Do you know?' he began at last, 'I must have dreamed it was winter and time to go to sleep, and I must have buried myself in my dream. I woke up in the snuggest hole you can imagine, tucked in so comfortably that it seemed a pity to disturb myself. But I felt hungry, which was odd, as I never feel hungry in the winter. So I pulled myself together and got out of my lovely hole and found myself in the garden once more. Whatever shall I do next! I've heard of people *walking* in their sleep, but never *burying* themselves.'

'Do you really bury yourself every winter?' asked the Dog.

'Of course I do, and I stay buried till the spring. I sleep half the year and wake half the year like every other tortoise.'

The pets looked more cheerful. There was something friendly about Tortoise as he laughed at himself, and they were glad he had not stayed for ever in the deep, dark hole. If he was to be asleep all the winter, it wouldn't be so bad. They could have dear Mrs Candy all to themselves on the long winter evenings.

'What can you do as well as bury yourself and eat lettuce?' asked the Cat.

'I can tell stories.'

'Tell us one now,' said everyone.

'Yes, if you like.'

'What kind of stories do you tell?' asked the Dog.

'I tell stories about anything that takes my fancy,' said Tortoise. 'Animals and birds and strange things that happen in strange lands.'

But Mrs Candy made them wait for the story till they had eaten their dinner, and then she washed Tortoise's shell and polished it with a spot of furniture cream. Shellover behaved very well while this was going on, making polite remarks

14

to the pets, and thanking Mrs Candy for her care and trouble.

'We don't mind Tortoise being here just in the summer if you still go on liking us best,' said the Dog to Mrs Candy.

'But of course I like you best!' said Mrs Candy in a surprised voice. 'I've known *you* since you were a fat little puppy, and *you* since you were a new-born kitten with a face like a pansy, and *you* since you were round balls of fluff, and *you* since you were a golden-brown calf. I've only known Shellover the Tortoise since this morning. I can't be as fond of him as I am of you. But I think we shall all like having someone different in the family who can tell stories.'

'And who sleeps all the winter,' added the Cat.

'Yes, and who sleeps all the winter. He will be my child in the summer and you will be my children all the year round.'

When Tortoise was clean and shining, he settled himself on the grass under the apple tree, and the pets and Mrs Candy arranged themselves comfortably around. The Hens perched in a row on the Cow's back as they could listen better that way. Everyone wondered what the first story would be about, and they sat quietly without moving a paw or a whisker. Only the Cat gave a little purr of pleasure when Shellover the Tortoise began by saying:

'My first story is called THE CAT VISITOR. Once upon a time . . .'

The Cat Visitor

ONCE upon a time a poor old man was sweeping his floor with a broom, sighing to himself as he swept. 'Oh dear,' he sighed. 'How cold it is tonight! How my back aches when I bend it! How hard life is when you are old and tired and haven't much money!'

'But this is Saturday night,' he thought and smiled, so that his thin, brown face was creased and crumpled like the skin of a withered apple. 'Saturday night, the one night in the week when I have a good supper of meat, and a bowl of bread and milk just before I go to bed. There's nothing like a bowl of bread and milk to warm a man and send him into a sound sleep.'

He was just propping the broom up in its corner, when he thought he heard a faint cry outside the door. The wind was howling in the chimney and the rain was beating on the window, and the cry was so faint that he could not be sure he had really heard it.

He stood still and listened. The cry came again, louder

than before. The old man hobbled to the door and opened it a little way. In came a mighty blast of wind and a flurry of rain and a thin, black cat.

She was a miserable-looking creature, with thin legs and a thin body and a tail like a black boot-lace. But she had the strength to mew and to rub her wet, cold self round the old man's ankles.

The old man dried his soaking visitor with a towel and went to the cupboard for a jug of milk. He filled a saucer and set it on the floor. The cat sprang to the saucer with a growl and lapped the milk noisily, leaving the saucer white and empty. She did not seem grateful, but mewed louder than before, looking up at the old man's face and then at the cupboard, with large, green eyes.

'Why, you're starving, you poor creature,' said the old man, filling the saucer again and adding a crumbled slice of bread to make the milk more satisfying. The saucer was emptied in a twinkling, and the mewing began once more, louder than ever. Once again the jug was brought out and the saucer filled and more bread added, only to be emptied in a few seconds. The more the cat drank, the thirstier she seemed to get.

'There's hardly enough left for my bread and milk' thought the old man, peering into the jug, 'and only a crust of bread. She may as well have the lot.' He emptied the jug into the saucer, draining the last drop, and crumbled the crust. When this, too, had vanished, the cat licked her lips and gazed hungrily round the room. Then she lifted her head and sniffed the air. She lashed her tail from side to side. The fur on her back bristled. She could smell the mutton chop that was in the cupboard, the old man's weekly treat.

The piercing mewing began again. The cat scratched at the cupboard door, looked over her shoulder at the old man, and then scratched again as if in a frenzy. Her eyes shone like green lamps. The old man could bear it no longer. He went to the cupboard, opened the door, and cut a piece off one end of the chop and gave it to her. She gulped it down and began to scratch with more energy than before, mewing pitifully.

'We'll go halves, that's fair as I'm hungry too,' said the old man, dividing what was left of the meat into two pieces and giving the cat one. But the cat's half vanished before he could shut the door, and the mewing went on so loudly that the old man gave up his own half to his visitor.

The meat finished, the cat still prowled up and down, mewing and looking up at him. She knew there was still the bone on the shelf. Now the old man had hoped to save at least the bone and boil it up later to make a drop of broth, but he could not shut his ears to the pitiful cries, or shut his eyes against the thin, bootlace of a tail and the great pleading eyes. He gave her the bone and she pounced on it and gnawed it with her sharp teeth, till it, too, was gone.

Then, at last, the mewing stopped as if the cat knew there was nothing left. She walked lightly to the hearth and sat down by the fender. As she washed her paws and re-arranged her damp fur, paying special attention to the ruff round her neck and to her bedraggled tail, the old man noticed that she was not the half-starved bag of bones he had thought. Her fur was thick and soft and her whiskers fierce and majestic. Even her tail now fluffed out to twice its previous size.

The fire was a small one as wood was hard to get in bad weather. When the cat had finished washing herself she began to shiver. Her whole body shook and her pointed teeth chattered. She crouched as near to the fire as she could get.

'You're in a bad way, pussy,' said the old man, whose own hands were stiff and blue with cold. 'I'll throw on another log.'

As the flames leapt and danced, the cat stopped shivering. She lay on her side and warmed her front. Then she rolled over and warmed her back. She waved her paws and lazily flapped her tail. Her mouth appeared to smile and from her throat came a deep, rich purr.

The old man was delighted. The flames crackled and the clock ticked and the visitor purred. How cosy he felt, and how peaceful and how contented! He quite forgot how hungry he was.

When the log was burned away and the flames died down the cat began to shiver again, and the chattering of her teeth was as loud as the ticking of the clock. The old man fetched the last two logs in the box, and soon the deep, rich purring began. They sat together, enjoying the glowing warmth.

It was after midnight when the old man went to bed, tucking the blankets snugly round himself and trying not to think of the empty cupboard. He thought of his visitor instead. Why, she might have starved to death if he hadn't given her a good meal.

Presently he felt something land on his bed and saw two green eyes shining. The cat wriggled her way under the bed-clothes and settled herself against his chest. She purred, and marked time with her front paws as cats do when they are sleepy and happy. The old man had been feeling chilly, even under the blankets, but once the cat had got comfortably

21

settled he felt a warmth creeping through him, from top to toe, and he soon fell into a deep sleep.

Next morning, the two of them woke late. The wind had dropped and the sun was shining on a light powdering of snow. There was nothing in the house to eat, so there was

no breakfast to get ready, and no more wood, so there was no fire to light.

The cat ran to the door and lifted her paw and mewed gently, asking to be let out. The old man opened the door and she stepped out into the sunshine.

'You don't look like the same cat,' he said. 'You seem

fatter. You hold your head as proudly as if you were a queen. Your fur shines and your eyes are like jewels.'

He had never before heard a cat speak, but he was not surprised when she looked back over her shoulder and said clearly:

'I have drunk your milk and eaten your bread and finished your meat and used up your last logs. Why don't you drive me away and slam the door?'

'Drive you away! Slam the door!' repeated the old man, in a puzzled voice. 'Why should I do that? You were cold and wet and hungry. Now you are warm and dry and satisfied. We were strangers, you and I. Now we are friends.' He bent down and stroked her furry back.

'Good-bye, my friend, good-bye!'

She ran along the path, jumped over the wall, and disappeared among the trees. It was some time later that the old man realized she had left no footprints in the powdery snow.

The cottage seemed empty and lonely, so he decided to tidy it up and occupy his mind with other things. He opened the cupboard and took out the empty milk jug to wash it. But it felt strangely heavy. It was empty no longer, filled to the brim with rich, creamy milk. The plate, too, was no longer bare. A thick, tempting mutton chop lay on it. Nearby was a loaf of bread, crisply baked and smelling delicious. The log box, standing in the corner, was piled high with logs of various sizes.

Soon the fire was blazing, the meat sizzling in the pan, and a bowl of bread and milk standing in the hearth. That night, when the old man went to bed and pulled up the blankets, the same warmth crept from head to foot, lulling him to sleep.

For the rest of his life, the cupboard always contained food and there were logs in the corner. The black cat never came again though sometimes, when the old man sat nodding by the fire, he heard not only the crackling of the fire and the ticking of the clock, but the deep purring of his friend.

The New Shoes

JENNY and Penny were sisters. They had blue eyes and long, fair plaits which a grown-up had to plait for them. They lost so many hair ribbons, white ones and blue ones and tartan ones, that they usually had their plaits finished off with rubber bands. They just wore ribbons for best.

Sometimes Jenny and Penny went away without their mother and stayed with their grandmother, who lived by the sea. They liked staying with granny very much, and they liked playing on the beach, and paddling, and digging in the sand. But they liked going home when the holiday was over, and telling their mother all their adventures.

One summer, Jenny and Penny went to stay with granny as usual. Their mother took them in the train and stayed one night before she went back home. When she said good-bye, she gave them each a new pair of beach shoes. The beach shoes were white with rubber soles, and they fastened with blue buttons. There was a blue edge to the strap, which made them pretty.

'Take care of them,' said their mother. 'Take care of your new beach shoes. It doesn't matter if they get wet because they will soon dry again, but please, please try not to lose them.'

'Of course we won't lose them,' said Jenny, 'they're so pretty.'

'We couldn't lose them if we tried!' said Penny.

'Well, don't try!' said their mother. 'You managed to lose a bucket last summer, and a bathing cap, and several spades. So just be very careful.'

'We were younger then,' said Jenny. 'We're sensible now.'

When their mother had said good-bye and gone back home to look after their father, grandmother got ready to go shopping.

'Would you like to come to the shops with me?' she said. 'Or would you rather go straight to the beach? I'll come down later when I've packed up our picnic.'

'We'd like to go straight to the beach, please,' said Jenny and Penny.

'Don't go farther than the long breakwater,' said granny, 'and then I shall know where you are. I'll bring your towels and bathing things when I come. Just take your spades and buckets.'

So granny went shopping with her basket, and Jenny and Penny ran down the lane to the sea. The beach was only five minutes away and when they got there they found they were the very first children. There was no one else in sight. There were no footmarks on the sand except the narrow, pointed prints the seagulls had made. The sea was calm. The waves broke gently with a tiny frill of foam and a soft 'sh'.

The little girls sat down and took off their new beach shoes. The buttons were rather stiff as the shoes were new, and Penny wriggled one foot out without undoing the strap.

'We must put them somewhere safe,' said Jenny. 'You know what mother said.'

'Yes, we must,' agreed Penny. 'Somewhere very safe. Shall we put them on the top of this big rock?'

'Oh no! Everyone could see them if they were on a rock. Someone might take them. They might think we had forgotten them.'

'Let's make a circle in the sand and put them in the middle. We might write our names in the sand beside them.'

'But a dog might snatch one up and run off with it.'

'Shall we take them with us and just lay them near us wherever we are playing? Then we can keep an eye on them.'

'That's what we did with our new buckets last year, and the sea took one away when our backs were turned. Do you remember? We saw it bobbing up and down in the water right out of reach.'

'Oh I do! We kept throwing stones at it but we never hit it. I think we'd better put our shoes on and play in them. They'll be safe on our feet.'

'No, don't let's do that,' said Jenny, wriggling her bare toes in the sand. 'Bare feet are much nicer. Anyhow, I want to paddle, don't you?'

'Yes, I do. I want to paddle this very minute. I nearly wish we hadn't got new shoes. They are such a bother.'

'I know,' said Jenny. 'We'll bury them. That's safe as safe. Come on, Penny.'

'What a good idea!' said Penny, as they dug a hole with

their spades, throwing up showers of sand. 'Don't dig it too deep or water will come in the bottom and then they'll be all damp and nasty to put on for going home.'

'This is deep enough. Let's put them in. How nicely they fit! Now we can cover them over.'

When they had finished covering them up there was a mound of sand over the hole.

'We must flatten this mound out,' said Penny. 'Someone might wonder what it was and start digging to find out. Let's spread the sand evenly and pat it down.'

They smoothed and spread and patted till there was no mound left; just a flat piece of sand.

'Now we can paddle!' shouted Jenny. 'Come on! I'll be in before you!'

The sea was cold at first and they both said 'OO!' but after a time it didn't feel cold any more.

'Isn't it warm?' said Penny.

'Boiling hot!' said Jenny.

They found a clear, interesting pool beside a big rock, shaped like a half moon. It was fringed with green ribbons of seaweed, and a few pink ones too. A crab lived under the seaweed. He came out and walked sideways over the sandy floor. Then he went back behind the green and pink curtains.

'Let's have the pool for our own,' said Penny. 'We can keep anything we find in it, and show them to granny when she comes.'

They poked about in the other little pools. Jenny caught three shrimps in her bucket and tipped them into the special pool. Penny found a starfish and they both found shells. Jenny found a hermit crab, too, a little, soft, pale crab without a shell of his own, who lived in a cockle shell.

It seemed no time before granny appeared, with the beach bag and the picnic basket.

'Granny! Granny!' they cried, running to meet her. 'May we bathe now, this very minute?'

'Yes, if you like,' said granny, taking the bathing suits out of the beach bag. Penny's was red and Jenny's was blue, and they both had white bathing caps. They could hardly wait while granny stuffed their plaits under their caps. Sometimes they fussed and said their caps were too tight and hurt them, but today they did not grumble. It was the very first bathe that summer.

Soon they were rolling and splashing in the sea, trying to swim, trying to float, and swallowing mouthfuls of very salt water.

When granny called 'Time to come out!' they came at once, though it felt as if they'd only been in two minutes. They had promised their mother to be good, so they didn't even beg for half a minute more.

Granny rubbed them down with the striped beach towels, which felt rough and sandy. When they were dressed, they put on their jerseys and ran to the big break-water and back to stop their teeth chattering.

'We're not a bit cold,' they explained to granny. 'We're really hot. But our teeth always chatter when we've had a bathe.'

The picnic was lovely, with all their favourite things to eat, and even a chocolate blancmange each in a little paper case.

The sun got hotter and hotter, and granny sat and knitted while they improved their pool. They made it deeper with their spades, and found more things to live in it. Penny found

a spider crab and some more shrimps. Jenny found a prickly sea-urchin and a tiny, pale pink jelly-fish.

When it was time to go back to tea, the tide was coming in, and the pool would soon be part of the great sea.

'We'll find it again tomorrow,' said Jenny, 'and see if any of the things are still there.'

As they dried their feet and rubbed the sand off them, granny suddenly said:

'Children! Wherever did you put your new beach shoes?'

'Don't worry, granny,' said Penny. 'They're very safe.'

'We spent ages and ages deciding what to do with them,' said Jenny. 'They're safe as safe. We buried them.'

'Buried them!' said granny. 'But where?'

'Oh, just somewhere near by.'

'Did you mark the place?'

'Oh no, granny. If we'd marked the place someone might have dug them up. It was a very, very secret place.'

'Then please find it as quickly as you can.'

Jenny and Penny ran up and down and round and round.

'It was near this rock.'

'Or maybe near this one.'

'But we hadn't come far from where we sat down first.'

'No, but we walked farther looking for a good place.'

'This may be it. The sand looks rough.'

'Or here. I'll dig here, and you dig there.'

They dug and dug like two dogs looking for a bone they had buried, or two squirrels wondering where they had hidden their nuts. Soon the beach was covered with small piles of sand. Granny dug too, using her hands because she hadn't a spade.

'I think we'll give it up,' said granny at last. 'You can try again tomorrow.'

'We did really mean to be sensible,' said Penny.

'We were really too sensible,' said Jenny. 'We found too safe a place.'

'Never mind,' said granny, giving them both a kiss. 'I can see that you did your best. Now you'll have to walk home barefoot like Irish tinkers!'

They never found the new beach shoes, though the girls sometimes had another search for them. They stayed hidden.

Granny bought them another pair each, dark blue and not so pretty, but there were no buttons. They just slipped on and off.

They never bothered to hide *these* shoes. They put them down just anywhere and they were always safe and sound when they were wanted. No dog ran away with them, and they were never swept out to sea.

Granny told mother about the shoes in a letter. When mother read the letter, she said: 'Oh dear! Oh dear! What will those children lose next?' Then, as she couldn't be really

cross, she began to laugh instead, and she made up this
poem about them. Here is the poem :

> Jenny and Penny
>   Had new shoes each.
> They wanted to keep them
>   Safe on the beach.
>
> They dug a hole
>   And hid them inside,
> And they've never found them
>   Though they've tried and tried !
>
> Sea, if you find them
>   With your long, green hand,
> Toss them safely
>   On to the sand.

Pineapple Polly
and the Lion Cub

THE Lion Cub peeped between the tall grasses that tickled his nose. He was the colour of sand, with soft fur and a friendly face. When he was older, he would have a glorious mane like his father, the King of Beasts. He saw the village where the black people lived. He saw their huts with mud walls and thatched roofs. He saw their fires and their cooking pots and their drums and their water jars. He saw the people too, doing their daily work. And he saw the children playing and laughing and getting into everyone's way.

The Lion Cub liked the children better than the men and women, because he was only young himself, and liked playing better than working. The child he watched more than the others was a little girl with black curls tied in a bunch on the top of her head, like the tuft on a pineapple. Her name was Pineapple Polly.

Pineapple Polly often played with a grass ball. She threw it high in the air and caught it again, and when she missed, and the ball rolled away among the bushes, she just laughed and ran after it.

The Lion Cub wanted to play with Pineapple Polly, and especially to play with her grass ball. He was sure that he could jump in the air and catch it in his mouth when she threw it to him. But he was afraid to walk into the clearing and try to make friends. He knew that her father and the other men did not like lions. They hunted them with bows and arrows and knives, and some of them slept on a mat made of lion skin. He did not want to be made into a lion-skin mat, not even if Pineapple Polly herself slept on him.

'I must persuade her to come with me into the forest,' said the Lion Cub. 'There we can play with the grass ball together, no one will mind. I will make my voice as soft as a pigeon's and see what I can do.'

He waited till Pineapple Polly had had her supper and been put to bed at sunset in her mud hut. Her father and mother sat down by the fire with their friends. Her father was smoking a pipe and her mother was spinning. The Lion Cub crept up behind the hut, where no one could see him, and sang as softly as he could:

> 'Pineapple Polly, come away!
> Pineapple Polly, come and play!
> I'll give you a shell
> With a rainbow inside.
> Come away! Come away!'

Pineapple Polly would have liked a rainbow shell all of her own but she did not care for the voice of the stranger. So she called out:

37

'Be off! Your voice is too harsh! You frighten me!'

The next day the Lion Cub went to see the Ju-Ju man, who could make magic. He brought him a present of a red lily, as he knew it was no good asking for advice unless he paid for it in advance.

'Ju-ju man,' he said, bowing low. 'How can I make my voice sweet?'

'Go and eat honey,' said the Ju-ju man, sticking the red lily, which was already fading, in his fuzzy black hair.

So the Lion Cub went to the wild bees and stole a great piece of their honeycomb. He ate every scrap and licked the last sticky bits off his paws. Then he crept up behind Pineapple Polly's hut, and sang:

'Pineapple Polly, come away!
Pineapple Polly, come and play!
I'll show you a cave
 Where you can hide.
Come away! Come away!'

Pineapple Polly would have found a secret cave very useful, especially when her mother was looking for her to stir the soup or gather sticks for the fire. But she did not care for the voice of the stranger. So she called out:

'Be off! Your voice is too loud! You frighten me!'

The next day the Lion Cub went to see the Ju-ju man again. He brought him a present of a custard apple.

'Ju-ju man,' he said, bowing low. 'How can I make my voice soft?'

'Go and eat the furry leaves of the chi-chi plant,' said the Ju-ju man, taking a bite out of the custard apple, which was beginning to go bad.

So the Lion Cub hunted everywhere for the chi-chi plant and when he found it he ate as many of the furry leaves as he could manage. He had to chew them very small as they were difficult to swallow. Then he crept up behind Pineapple Polly's hut, and sang:

> 'Pineapple Polly, come away!
> Pineapple Polly, come and play!
> I'll thread coral beads
> On a plaited string.
> Come away! Come away!'

Pineapple Polly would have been very proud to wear a necklace of coral, and thought how pretty it would look on her dark skin, but she did not care for the voice of the stranger. So she called out:

'Be off! Your voice is too husky. You frighten me!'

The next day the Lion Cub went to see the Ju-ju man again. He brought him a present of a wild pear.

'Ju-ju man,' he said, bowing low. 'How can I make my voice clear?'

'Go up to the mountains and drink snow water,' said the Ju-ju man, pinching the wild pear, which felt hard and looked green

The Lion Cub toiled up the high, rocky mountain till his legs were tired and his paws were sore. When he came to the ice-cold stream made of melting snow water, he drank and drank, till the cold made his teeth ache. Then he ran down the mountain and crept up behind Pineapple Polly's hut, and sang:

> 'Pineapple Polly, come away!
> Pineapple Polly, come and play!
> I'll make you a bangle
> And a gold ring.
> Come away! Come away!'

Pineapple Polly could hardly resist the promise of a bangle *and* a gold ring. No little girl in the whole tribe had a bangle *and* a ring. But she did not care for the voice of the stranger. So she called out:

'Be off! Your voice is too shrill! You frighten me!'

The next day, the Lion Cub went to see the Ju-ju man again. He brought him a present of wood for his fire.

'Ju-ju man,' he said, bowing low. 'How can I make my voice low?'

'Go and get some mud,' said the Ju-ju man, frowning at the wood, which was damp, 'and make a compress of leaves and mud and wrap it round your throat.'

So the Lion Cub found some mud and spread it on a big leaf and wrapped the leaf round his throat. Then he crept behind Pineapple Polly's hut, and sang:

'Pineapple Polly, come away!
Pineapple Polly, come and play!
If you are sad
I will dance and sing.
Come away! Come away!'

Pineapple Polly sat up on her mat when she heard this. The stranger sounded so kind. She was not often sad, it was true, but it would be comforting to have someone to cheer her up if she were. But even then she did not really care for the voice of the stranger. So she called out:

'Be off! Your voice is too rough. It frightens me!'

The next day the Lion Cub went to see the Ju-ju man for the last time. He brought him a present of a fish.

'Ju-ju man,' he said, bowing low. 'How can I make my voice tender?'

The Ju-ju man was getting bad tempered because he did not like being bothered with questions every day, and the presents had been poor ones. Why, even the fish smelt rotten. So he gave bad advice instead of good. He said:

'Go and eat thistledown!' and he added, under his breath: 'I hope it chokes you!'

The Lion Cub searched everywhere for thistledown and when he found some, he did his best to swallow it. But it tickled his throat and he could only manage a very little. Then he crept up behind Pineapple Polly's hut and tried to sing, only the thistledown stuck in his throat and made him cough. He coughed so loudly that all the men in the village came running after him, waving their bows and arrows, and even the little boys followed him with sticks and stones.

They very nearly caught him and made him into a lion-skin mat for someone to sleep on, but he just managed to get away in time because he knew the forest better than they, and he had four legs to run with instead of two.

When the men and the boys found they could not catch the Lion Cub they went back to the village, boasting that they had driven away a large, fierce lion.

Pineapple Polly ran out of her hut when she heard the commotion going on, and she caught a glimpse of the Lion Cub. He did not look large or fierce at all. He looked small

and friendly. So she stayed behind and watched to see what would happen next. When all was quiet, the Lion Cub came softly from under a bush and sat down and licked his paws. He coughed a little because the thistledown still tickled his throat. Then he whimpered because he was young and lonely and the rough voices of the men had frightened him.

'Poor Lion Cub!' thought Pineapple Polly. 'He has no one to play with. What can I do to make him happy? I know, I'll give him my grass ball.'

So she went to the hut and brought the grass ball back, and threw it towards the Lion Cub. When he saw it rolling along the ground towards him, he picked it up in his mouth and ran gaily off into the forest, to the secret cave that only he knew about, and there he played with his ball, and played with his ball, and had fun.

He did not go to the Ju-ju man for any more advice, and he kept away from Pineapple Polly's hut in the evenings, though he would like to have thanked her for his lovely present. But he never forgot her. He liked her so much, especially the bunch of curls on the top of her little black head.

Bristles from the
Witch's Broom

THE village of Little Willow was so small that everyone in it knew everyone else very well. When a visitor arrived at Cherry Tree Farm, everyone knew what she looked like and what luggage she had brought. By the next day, they even knew that her name was Mrs Crabapple.

Mrs Crabapple was no ordinary woman. Her clothes were odd to begin with, as she wore a cloak and a high, pointed black hat. Her nose was rather like a beak and her eyes were bright under bushy eyebrows.

When the farmer's wife went shopping in the village, her friends stopped her and asked questions about the new visitor.

'Is she as odd as she looks?' they asked.

'She's a polite, harmless person,' replied the farmer's wife. 'Really very little trouble to look after. Of course she has her little ways, but who hasn't? She insists on her cat sleeping on her bed at night and she's always talking to the creature. And she's very fond of vinegar – she even takes it on her porridge. But then she doesn't have sugar, so what I lose one way I gain the other.'

Robert Rake and his school friend Anna Jones were very interested in Mrs Crabapple. They peered into the window of the farmhouse when they went to fetch eggs for their mothers. They saw Mrs Crabapple with a plate of something hot and steaming in front of her, pouring vinegar over it with a contented look on her face. Her cat, black as coal, rubbed round the leg of her chair.

'I'm sure we're right,' said Anna, as they walked away.

'I'm nearly sure too,' said Robert. 'Did you tell your mother what you thought?'

'Yes, I did, and she laughed at me. She said old ladies often wore strange hats and did strange things. She told me not to mix up things I'd read in books with things in real life. Did you tell your mother?'

'Yes, and she laughed too. She said she was surprised I should believe such ridiculous nonsense.'

'But parents are so old,' went on Anna. 'They forget. Anyone can tell at a glance what Mrs Crabapple really is. There's the tall hat –'

'And the black cat –' went on Robert.

'And the cloak –'

'I'm going to find out if she keeps a broomstick in her bedroom. I suppose her books of spells are safely hidden away. It wouldn't do to leave them lying about.'

Mrs Crabapple liked the village of Little Willow. She roamed through the fields and woods, with her black cat trotting beside her, talking either to herself or to him. Anna found out that she *did* keep a broomstick in her bedroom, though, added the farmer's wife, 'I can't imagine why. She never sweeps up a hair or a crumb with it.'

One day, Mrs Crabapple called on the village builder, Mr Winks, and asked him if he would build her a house.

'With pleasure,' said Mr Winks. 'I know what you want exactly. A nice country cottage with roses round the door and a thatched roof.'

'Not at all,' said Mrs Crabapple, 'now what I have in mind –' but Mr Winks would not let her finish.

'I might have guessed, you prefer something more modern. Big windows – a flat roof for sun-bathing – a swimming pool –' but he could see from the frown on her face that this was not much better.

'Mr Winks,' said Mrs Crabapple sternly, 'is this house for *you* to live in, or for *me*? I have all my plans ready. Get a large sheet of paper and make notes while I explain.'

As Mrs Crabapple explained he opened his eyes wider and wider and licked his pencil in a worried way.

'There you are,' said Mrs Crabapple at last. 'I think that's everything. All you have to do is to get on with the job.'

Mr Winks put his pencil back behind his ear.

'I've been a builder in this village for nearly fifty years and I've never heard of such a house. I just can't do it. My pride won't let me. Everybody for miles round would laugh at me. They'd think I was mad, and they'd be right, too.'

'Whatever is wrong?' asked Mrs Crabapple. 'It's a very ordinary house, the kind I've always lived in.'

'What is wrong? Pretty well everything. You want a ROUND house with ONE chimney and a MOAT all round. You don't want any hot water and the stairs have to twist like a corkscrew and you must see the moon rise from your bedroom window. It can't be done.'

Mrs Crabapple, very annoyed, flounced out of Mr Winks's office and hurried down the road. On the way, she stopped to see three men mending a stone wall. One, with a white beard, was resting on the grass; another, with black whiskers, was chewing a straw; a third, a young boy, was fitting a stone into position. She asked their names and the name of their master.

'I'm Old Tom,' said white beard.

'I'm Uncle Tom,' said black whiskers.

'I'm Young Tom,' said the boy, 'and we work for ourselves.'

'Then you can work for me for a change,' said Mrs Crabapple. 'You've only got to do what I tell you, and I will pay you well. And you must all work' she added, looking disapprovingly at Old Tom and Uncle Tom, 'or you won't be paid.'

The three Toms started work the next day and they were so proud of building a real house, instead of just mending walls, that they worked well. There were no rests on the grass and no straw-chewing.

Robert and Anna watched whenever they passed that way. They saw the round wall rising higher and higher and the one chimney beginning to sprout out of the roof. They saw the moat getting deeper and deeper. At last the house was finished and the three Toms, well content, went home.

Mrs Crabapple hired the farm cart and drove to her new house with her luggage. Half the village were watching as she crossed the moat by the bridge, then disappeared through the door.

The next day, on their way to school, Robert and Anna

found time to pass the new house. Mrs Crabapple was painting some words on the gate. They read the rather smudged letters: THE SPIDER'S WEB.

'It's another proof,' said Robert. 'No ordinary person would choose a name like that.'

'Of course they wouldn't,' agreed Anna. 'It's just as we thought from the beginning. Mrs Crabapple is a witch.'

After a while, Robert and Anna and everyone else in the village got used to seeing Mrs Crabapple hurrying by, her black coat flying and her black cat at her heels. But they could not help wondering what she was *really* like. What did she do in her queer, round house? How old was she? Where did she buy her pointed hats?

Mrs Crabapple said 'Good morning' to anyone she met, and paid her bills at the shops, but she made no friend. No one ever visited her or went inside THE SPIDER'S WEB.

People were put off by the state of the garden, which was thick with nettles and thistles. The path that led from the gate and over the bridge to the front door was grown over with weeds. Even the postwoman, who feared neither bulls nor snowdrifts, would not push her way through. She stopped at the gate and blew loudly on a whistle, which brought Mrs Crabapple out to meet her.

People passing at night were surprised at the number of bats flitting over the garden, and the harsh screeching of the owls.

The only cheerful thing about the place was Mrs Crabapple herself, who had a nice smile and tripped along as if she hadn't a care in the world.

Robert and Anna longed to go inside the house and see what it was like. But they could not think of a good excuse for calling. Then Robert suggested they might offer to tidy the garden.

'Oh Robert,' said Anna, 'supposing she says yes! Whatever could we do with all those giant thistles and stinging nettles? It would take us all the holidays and more.'

'Well,' said Robert, 'we can offer. Then she'll see that it's an impossible job. Come on. Let's go now.'

Feeling a little shy, they opened the squeaking gate and began to make their way through the jungle. But, to their surprise, no harm came to their bare legs. The thistles did not prick and the nettles did not sting. When they reached the front door, Mrs Crabapple opened it before they could knock and Cinders, the cat, rubbed himself gently round their ankles.

'Cinders likes children and never scratches,' said Mrs Crabapple. 'Shake hands with Robert and Anna, Cinders.'

Cinders offered a velvet paw.

'How did you know our names?' asked Anna.

'Oh, I know a great deal about you both. I know where the hollow oak is, and what you've hidden there, and where you buried the dead bird, and what your secret language is. But you mustn't mind my knowing. I never tell other people's secrets.'

'Do you know why we've called today?' asked Robert.

'Yes, you've called to offer to tidy my garden. But don't worry. I like my garden just as it is. I planned it to be like this. My favourite drink is nettle tea, so I shouldn't like the nettles to be cut down.'

'But what about the thistles?' put in Robert.

'They are my favourite vegetable. I am never ill. I never have been ill, I never intend to be ill, and I feel sure my good health is due to my diet.'

'Then we'd better go home,' said Anna sadly. She was glad when Mrs Crabapple said quickly:

'Please don't go yet. Would you like to see my house? I've lived here a month and no one has called yet.'

'Oh, we'd love to,' said the children, crossing their fingers as a safeguard against magic. They had arranged this earlier on.

They saw many signs of magic as they went about the house, but they did not feel at all frightened. Anna knocked the broomstick down, by mistake, and it stood itself back in its corner.

They looked at the large cauldron, in the kitchen, with a bright fire burning under it. Robert peeped inside, but saw nothing more alarming than gallons of boiling water.

'This modern craze for hot-water pipes and taps is absurd,' said Mrs Crabapple. 'What's wrong with a good iron caul-

dron? No pipes to burst when it freezes. A comfortable sound of bubbling water while you do your work. You can cook your dinner, heat your bath, boil your washing, anything you like. My family has believed in cauldrons for many years.'

A grown-up person would have been shocked at the muddle everywhere, but the children loved a hugger-mugger and wished their own tidy homes were more like this one. There were the oddest things in the oddest places. A row of boots stood on the mantelpiece. There were peacock feathers stuck behind the pictures. There were boxes, books, clothes, fir cones, and cat's saucers all over the floor.

'You must have some sweets before you go,' said Mrs Crabapple, offering a tin of tempting sweets. The children mumbled 'No thank you – no, really – we won't have any.'

'All children like sweets. Just fill your pockets and don't be shy.'

'We needn't *eat* them,' whispered Robert in Anna's ear. They had never before seen such lovely sweets. Each was a tiny toy or person made of coloured sugar. There were Red Indians and drums and dolls and rings. There were engines and flowers and stars, all clear as barley sugar.

They thanked Mrs Crabapple, stroked Cinders, and crossed the moat by the bridge.

'Of course we can't eat any,' said Robert.

'Of course not,' agreed Anna. 'It might be dangerous.'

'It's a pity we can't eat just one,' went on Robert, looking very carefully at a red engine.

'Yes, it's a pity that even one would be a risk,' said Anna, licking a yellow canary with the tip of her tongue.

'They are sure to be bewitched. We might turn into anything.'

'We might be spiders or toads for the rest of our lives.'

They walked on in silence, Anna tormented by the sweetness of her first taste. Robert nibbled the top of the engine-

54

funnel and sighed. Their mouths watered and they could not bear to throw the sweets away.

Anna gave in first.

'I'm going to eat the head off this canary,' she said firmly. 'Then, if nothing happens, I'm going to eat the rest of it.' Crunch! The head was gone and Anna was still her usual self.

'Then I shall eat my red engine.'

Never before had they tasted such sweets. Never had sugar melted so smoothly on their tongues. One by one the sweets disappeared as they nibbled and sucked and admired and popped in just one more.

'If I do change into something in the night it will have been worth it,' said Anna contentedly.

'You're more likely to be sick in the night,' said Robert.

But nothing terrible happened. They were not sick or sorry. The next time Mrs Crabapple offered them sweets, they took them straight off, without even crossing their fingers.

'I'm so glad you are not going to keep your fingers crossed all the time you're in my house,' remarked Mrs Crabapple.

'Why?' asked Robert.

'Because you might get pins and needles.'

Until now the children had told no one about their visits to THE SPIDER'S WEB, but in the end they told their best friends about the cauldron and the books of spells and the other queer things. But their friends just laughed at their stories. They simply didn't believe a word.

'Don't tell such fibs!'

'What on earth have you been reading?'

'What utter nonsense!'

'You made it all up!'

But Robert and Anna found a way of getting even with the children who made fun of them. They brought a bag of barley sugar fishes to school, that Mrs Crabapple had made, and ate them at playtime. The others gathered round and begged for 'just one!' But Robert and Anna shook their heads.

'Sorry we can't offer you any,' they said. 'These sweets are like our stories about Mrs Crabapple – just make believe – they're not *real* sweets, you know. So you couldn't really eat them, could you?'

The Flood

THE shed was near the house. It was dark because it had only one small window, and that was covered with cobwebs. There were some tools in the shed, a spade and a rake and a hoe, and a pile of old sacks. There was something else as well, that not many people knew about. If you stood quite still in the shed, without moving a hand or a foot, you could hear the crackle of straw and perhaps a tiny cry.

The crackle of straw and the cry came from a box standing in a corner. In the box were a mother cat and her three new-born kittens. The cat's name was Minnie and her kittens were named One, Two, and Three. When they were big and could wash themselves and drink milk from a saucer, they would go to homes of their own. Then someone would give them proper names. But One, Two, and Three did very well to start with.

Sometimes a dog barked.

'What is that?' asked One, his little legs shaking.

'It is only Prince, the dog,' purred Minnie. 'He is taking care of us. He barks when he sees a stranger coming.'

Sometimes a door banged.

'What is that?' mewed Two, shuddering like a jelly.

'It is only the wind blowing the door shut,' purred Minnie. 'Now the wind won't get into our snug bed.'

Sometimes the coalman tipped the coal out with a sound like thunder.

'What is that?' cried Three, hiding her face in her mother's fur.

'It is only the coalman,' purred Minnie. 'His coal will make the kitchen fire blaze and burn. I will take you into the kitchen for a treat, when you are bigger, if you are very good.'

A lady named Mrs Plum lived in the kitchen. She wore a white apron. Every day she brought Minnie's meals to her, in a blue dish. When Minnie had finished her food, the dish was as clean as if it had been washed.

One night, when the kittens were fast asleep, curled like furry balls beside their mother, a storm blew up. The door and window of the shed rattled. The rain fell in floods on the roof. There were terrible claps of thunder and bright, zigzag flashes of lightning. Even Minnie felt frightened. The river ran at the bottom of the garden, on the other side of the garden wall, and she could hear it roaring by. It sounded like a fierce, growling animal.

'What is wrong? What has happened?' mewed One, Two, and Three.

'I do not know, my dears,' said Minnie. 'But we must go to sleep and not be frightened.'

But Minnie herself was very frightened and so were the three kittens. No one could get to sleep while the storm was raging.

The kittens were so young that their eyes were not yet

open. But Minnie's eyes shone like green lamps. She could see, under the door of the shed, a trickle of water. The trickle grew into a puddle. The puddle grew into a wave. The wave came nearer and nearer across the floor. Then it reached the box in the corner.

Minnie did not like water. She did not even like getting her paws wet on the wet grass. She was very, very frightened to see the water creeping under the door and spreading across the whole floor.

'If it gets any deeper,' she thought to herself, 'I shall take the kittens in my mouth, one at a time, and jump on to the wheelbarrow, and then up on to the shelf where the flower-pots are stacked. I don't think the water could get as high as that.'

The water flowed faster and faster under the door until it was inches deep. Just when Minnie was getting ready to take a kitten in her mouth and spring on to the wheelbar-row, and then on to the shelf, a strange thing happened. The wooden box began to move about. It was floating. It was floating like a boat.

There was a thick layer of straw in the bottom of the box and an old woollen jersey. The kittens stayed dry and warm while they floated in their bed. They did not mind at all be-cause they could not see the water as their eyes were shut.

Suddenly there was a clap of thunder and a great blast of wind. The door of the shed blew open with a bang. The water rushed in and the box swirled round and round. Then it floated out of the shed into the garden.

The river had risen so high that it swept over the garden wall. The box swished over the wall and sailed along the river which was now wide and deep like a sea. It was too dark to see exactly where they were going. Minnie cuddled

59

her babies close to her while the rain fell in torrents. The kittens were soon fast asleep, and though Minnie was sure she would never get a wink herself, she dozed off as well.

When morning came, they were in a watery world. There was water in front of them. Water behind. Water all round. Minnie did not know there could be so much water in one place. Strange things floated by. Branches of trees which had been torn off by the storm. Tables and chairs and pillows and cushions that had been washed out of houses. Sacks and straw and even a dog-kennel. Minnie was pleased to see that the kennel was empty.

Nothing stopped Minnie from bringing up her kittens as well as she could, so she washed them just as carefully as if they had been on dry land. When she had finished One's face, he mewed in an excited voice:

'I can see! I can see! I can see you and Two and Three and the water and everything!'

He frisked about with joy and Minnie was afraid he might fall out of the box.

Before long, Two and Three could see as well and they spent most of the day calling out:

'What's that? What's that? What's that?' or else: 'Why is the water shiny? Why is it brown?' and many other questions, some of which Minnie could not answer.

Though the kittens were well and happy, Minnie was worried. The kittens were fat as butter and could drink her warm milk whenever they wished. But there was nothing for *her* to eat, no milk – no fish – no liver. Nothing at all.

The other thing that worried her was that she could not bring her children up properly in a box floating on the water. How would they learn to lap milk from a saucer? Or walk upstairs? Or climb trees? Or catch mice? Minnie had

61

brought up so many families of kittens that she knew exactly how the job ought to be done.

Now that the rain had stopped the floods began to go down. The river was no longer wild and roaring. Hedges and bushes could be seen that had been under the water a few hours before. When the box drifted near the bank and was caught on the branches of a willow tree, Minnie knew what she must do.

Quick as a flash, she snatched up the nearest kitten who happened to be Two, and climbed up the tree with him. She dashed back for One and Three and the little family were soon perched on the damp, slippery branch of a willow, instead of cuddled in a floating cradle filled with straw.

'This is a horrid place!' mewed One.

'I shall fall into the water and be drowned!' mewed Two.

'How are we to sleep without a bed?' mewed Three.

Minnie was not comfortable herself as she was trying to look after three young kittens as well as hold on, but she did not approve of grumbling.

'The river is going down,' she said cheerfully. 'Tomorrow or the next day I shall carry you home, one at a time, in my mouth. Till then, you must be good kittens and do what I tell you.'

'Do you know the way home?' asked One. 'We must have floated a long way in our wooden box.'

Minnie was not certain that she *did* know the way, but she replied firmly:

'Of course I know the way. The river brought us here. I shall just follow the river and it will lead us home. Anyhow, all sensible cats know the way home. They never get lost.'

All day and all night Minnie took care of her kittens. She fed them and washed them and sang to them, and when they slept she kept them from falling off the branch. When they were awake and wanted to play, she told them stories. She told them about the red kitchen fire that ate black coal. She told them about mice with long tails who lived in holes and were fun to chase. She told them about dear Mrs Plum and her white apron and her warm, comfortable lap.

When the *next* morning came, the river had gone right down. The ground was wet and muddy, but it was not under water. They could see the path running along the river bank.

'I shall take one of you home now,' said Minnie.

'Take me!' 'No, me!' 'No, ME!' mewed the three kittens.

'I shall take Three first because she is the smallest,' said Minnie. 'Now One and Two, be brave and sensible and hold on tightly.'

'What will happen if we fall off?' asked One and Two.

'You would lose one of your nine lives,' said Minnie. 'Then you would have only eight left.'

She took little Three in her mouth, climbed down the tree to the ground, and ran off along the river bank. She felt sure she was going the right way and that every step was bringing her nearer home. The wet mud was cold and nasty to her feet, but she did not mind. If only her three kittens were safe in front of the kitchen fire, she would never mind anything again!

Little Three squirmed and squiggled and seemed to get heavier and heavier. When at last Minnie padded slowly through the gate and up the path to the back door, she could hardly drag one foot after the other.

'Miaow! Miaow!' she cried as loudly as she could. 'Miaow!'

In a second the door opened and there stood dear Mrs Plum in her white apron.

'Oh, Minnie! Minnie!' she cried, gathering Minnie and Three up in her arms, and not minding at all about the mud they left on her apron. 'I thought I should never see you again!'

At first Minnie purred loudly and smiled, but she knew the job was not yet finished. She began to kick and struggle till Mrs Plum put her down on the floor. Then she ran to the back door and mewed for it to be opened.

'I know,' said Mrs Plum. 'I understand. You must go back for the others. Wait a moment and I will come too, I'll just make Three safe and comfortable. I kept a bed ready for you all.'

There, on the hearth-rug, was another box with a soft blanket inside. Mrs Plum cuddled Three into the blanket, and Three sat and stared at the fire with round blue eyes. So *this* was the monster who ate black coal!

Mrs Plum put on her coat and hat and took a basket with a lid and opened the door. Minnie ran ahead so quickly that Mrs Plum could only just keep up. They were both tired when they got to the willow tree. Mrs Plum stood at the bottom while Minnie climbed up and found her two kittens cold and shivering, but quite safe.

'We've kept all our nine lives, Mother!' they called out.

'That's my good kittens!' said Minnie, carrying them down to the ground, where Mrs Plum stroked them and petted them and tucked them into the basket, which was lined with flannel. There was just room for Minnie as well. Then Mrs Plum carried the heavy basket home. She had to change hands when one arm ached.

When they were back in the warm kitchen, Mrs Plum gave Minnie a good meal. She had sardines and a dish of cornflakes and three saucers of milk. Then they all five settled down for a cosy afternoon by the fire. Mrs Plum knitted in her rocking chair, and the three kittens watched the red fire eating coal and stared at the brass rim of the fender and the plates on the dresser and all the other wonderful things.

They kept looking at Mrs Plum's ball of wool.

'I don't know why, but I should like to roll that ball of wool all over the floor,' said One.

'So should I!' said Two and Three.

'That would be very naughty of you indeed,' said Minnie. 'But I wanted to do just the same when I was a kitten.'

'And did you do it?' asked the three kittens.

'Yes, I'm afraid I did!' said Minnie.

She purred and smiled and dozed, as the clock ticked on the wall and the fire crackled and Mrs Plum clicked her knitting needles.

The Ugsome Thing

THERE was once a monster called the Ugsome Thing. He was round and fat and scaly and he had long teeth twisted like sticks of barley sugar. He lived in a castle and had many servants to wait on him. They had to clean his castle and cook his food and till his fields and tend his flocks and herds. Though they worked hard, he never paid them a penny in wages.

The Ugsome Thing had a magic power, and if he could make anyone lose his temper, that person became his slave and had to obey him.

At this time, the Ugsome Thing had all the servants he wanted except for one – he had not a good washerwoman. His clothes were often dirty and badly ironed. Now, as he went through the village near his castle, he passed a cottage garden which was full, on a Monday, of the whitest clothes he had ever seen. They were like snow, blowing and billowing on the line stretched between two apple trees. He decided to make the old woman who lived there come and do

his washing. It would be very simple. He only had to make her lose her temper and she would be in his power.

So one Monday morning, when her clothes-line was full of the whitest wash possible, he cut the line with his knife and the snowy clothes lay tumbled on the dirty grass. Surely *that* would make her lose her temper.

When the old woman saw what had happened, she came running out of the door, and instead of losing her temper she said quietly:

'Well! Well! Well! The chimney has been smoking this morning and I'm sure some smuts must have blown on to my washing, anyway. It will be a good idea to wash it again. How lucky that the line broke just this morning and no other!'

So she picked up armfuls of the dirty clothes and went back to the wash-house, singing as she went.

The Ugsome Thing was very angry and he gnashed his barley sugar teeth, but he soon thought of another idea to make her lose her temper.

On Tuesday the Ugsome Thing visited the old woman again. He saw that she had milked her cow, Daisy, and that the milk stood in a pan in the dairy. He turned the whole pan of milk sour. Surely *that* would make her lose her temper.

When the old woman saw the pan of sour milk she said:

'Well! Well! Well! Now I shall have to make it into cream cheese and that will be a treat for my grandchildren when they come to tea. They love having cream cheese on their scones. How lucky that the milk turned sour just today and no other!'

The Ugsome Thing was very angry and he gnashed his barley sugar teeth, but he soon thought of another idea to make her lose her temper.

On Wednesday the Ugsome Thing visited the old woman again. He turned all the hollyhocks in her garden into thistles, the red ones and the pink ones and the double yellow ones. She was very proud of her pretty garden. Surely *that* would make her lose her temper.

'Well! Well! Well!' said the old woman when she saw thistles growing by the wall instead of hollyhocks. 'I was going to pick a bunch of hollyhocks today for my friend's birthday, but now I shall make her a pin-cushion instead, and stuff it with thistledown.'

So she made a velvet pin cushion and stuffed it with thistledown and embroidered a flower on it. It looked nearly as pretty as the hollyhocks and lasted much longer.

'How lucky I am that I noticed all those thistles just today and no other,' she said, as she sewed up the pin-cushion.

The Ugsome Thing was very angry and gnashed his barley sugar teeth, but he soon thought of another idea to make her lose her temper.

On Thursday the Ugsome Thing stretched a piece of string across the stairs, hoping that the old woman would trip over it and fall. Surely that would make her lose her temper.

The old woman did fall, and hurt her knee, and had to hop on one leg to the shed to milk Daisy the cow.

'Well! Well! Well!' said the old woman. 'I can't do any housework today. I shall lie on the sofa and get on with my patchwork quilt. What a nice change that will be! I may even get it finished. How lucky I am that I tripped over just today, and no other!'

The Ugsome Thing was very angry and gnashed his barley sugar teeth, but he soon thought of another idea to make her lose her temper.

On Friday the Ugsome Thing visited the old woman again. He saw her going to the hen-house to collect the eggs. She had three white hens and they had each laid an egg. As she was walking past the apple tree, he flipped a branch in her face and she dropped the bowl and broke the eggs. Surely *that* would make her lose her temper.

'Well! Well! Well!' said the old woman. 'Now I shall have to have scrambled eggs for dinner and supper, and scrambled eggs are my favourite food. How lucky I am that the eggs broke just today and no other!'

Now the Ugsome Thing was very angry indeed and he gnashed his barley sugar teeth, but he soon thought of another idea to make her lose her temper. This idea was a very nasty one, because he was very, very angry indeed.

On Saturday the Ugsome Thing set the old woman's cottage on fire. Surely *that* would make her lose her temper. The flames shot up the walls and soon the thatched roof caught fire.

'Well! Well! Well!' said the old woman. 'That's the last of my old cottage. I was fond of it, but it was falling to pieces and the roof let in the rain and there were holes in the floor.' When the Ugsome Thing came along to see if the old woman had lost her temper, he found her busy baking potatoes in the hot ashes, and handing them round to the village children.

'Have a potato?' she said to the Ugsome Thing, holding one out on the point of a stick.

It smelled so good that the Ugsome Thing took it and crammed it into his mouth whole, because he was very greedy, and some of it went down the wrong way. He choked so hard with rage and hot potato that he burst like a balloon and there was nothing left but a piece of shrivelled, scaly,

greenish skin. A little boy threw it on the fire, thinking it was an old rag, and it burned with a spluttering yellow flame.

By this time, most of the people in the village were lining up to have a baked potato, and while they waited they planned how they could help the old woman.

'I'll build the walls of a new cottage,' said one.

'I'll make the roof,' said another.

'I'll put in the windows,' said a third.

'I'll paper the walls,' said a fourth.

'We'll give her a carpet – sheets – a blanket – a kettle –'
said the women. By the time all the potatoes were cooked
and eaten, her friends had promised the old woman all she
needed for a new cottage.

The new cottage was not old and tumbledown like the first one, but dry and comfortable with a sunny porch. Daisy had a new shed and the dog a new kennel. Only the cat was disappointed as there were no mice for her to chase. There were no holes for the mice to live in.

The Acorn Man

LONG ago, a little brother and sister lived with their father and mother in a cottage. They were very poor. They had hardly enough to eat and the children's arms and legs were as thin as sticks. Their clothes were covered with patches and darns, and the winter wind pinched them with icy fingers.

But they loved each other dearly, and they laughed more often than they cried. When they sat round the fire in the evenings, after their bowl of soup and slice of bread which was their supper, they looked at the pictures in the fire made by the glowing logs as they settled and crumbled.

'I see a fine wagon drawn by a pair of strong horses,' said their father.

'I see a great, billowy feather bed, big enough to keep us all warm,' said the mother.

'I see a sledge coming down a hill with Cherry and me on it,' said Dick, the boy.

'I see a tree laden with red apples', said Cherry.

There was no money to spare for such grand things as wagons or feather beds, and the children had to be content

75

with a rough board for a sledge, and a wrinkled apple as a treat, but these pictures made them feel happy and comfortable.

The children helped their parents as much as they could, but they were too young to do hard work. Dick could not dig, or cut down trees, or mend the roof. Cherry could not spin wool or knit socks, or bake bread.

But when the autumn came and the leaves began to fall, their father sent them into the forest with a sack to gather acorns. These were to be given to the pig who lived in a sty beside the cottage. They would help to keep him fat and contented during the long, cold winter.

The children set out after breakfast with the empty brown sack, and two slices of bread and two pieces of cheese in Dick's pocket. At first they sang and skipped about, dragging the sack behind them, but by the time they had reached the forest they were walking slowly and shuffling their feet. Even the empty sack had become a burden.

There were oak trees dotted about, here and there, but in one place several grew together. Here the children stopped, and began to scrabble among the dead leaves for the shining acorns.

'Here's one, and there's another!' said Dick. 'Oh, there are lots and lots.'

'This is a good place too,' said Cherry, 'but I wish they weren't all hidden under the leaves.'

They rolled back the mouth of the sack so they could easily drop the acorns inside. They smoked acorn pipes, for fun, as they worked. The acorns pattered into the sack, sometimes single ones, sometimes a handful.

'The bottom is hardly covered yet,' said Cherry sadly, peering inside.

'I'm starving,' said Dick. 'Shall we eat our dinner?'

'Let's each put a hundred in, and then stop for a rest. Surely two hundred more will cover the bottom. Come on, Dick!'

Cherry began counting under her breath as she dropped the acorns in:

'One—two—four—seven—nine—ten—eleven.'

Meanwhile, Dick was quicker. 'A hundred!' he soon said. 'How many have you?'

'Only seventy-nine.'

'I'll help you to finish. Here's eighty, eighty-one, eighty-two . . .'

They soon finished Cherry's hundred, and then they sat down on a tree-trunk and began to eat their dinner, taking small bites of bread and tiny nibbles of cheese, to make it seem more.

Dick finished first. He shook the crumbs out of his pocket, and also some odd treasures: a stub of pencil, some pins stuck into a cork, and a bit of string. While Cherry was still eating, he chose a large, dark acorn and a small round one with the cup still attached. He used the pins to fix the round acorn on top of the big one, for a head, and then added four pins for arms and legs. By licking the pencil and pressing hard, he made a face, and buttons down the front.

'How lovely!' said Cherry. 'An acorn man! Perhaps he'll help us to gather acorns.'

'Let's ask him,' said Dick, and he said politely:

'Will you help us, good little acorn man? The sack is big and the acorns are small.'

The little Acorn Man jumped out of Cherry's hand, bowed to the oak tree, and sang:

77

> 'Oak tree, oak tree,
> Hear when I call,
> Pitter-patter, pitter-patter,
> Let the acorns fall.'

At once there was a sound like the start of a hailstorm. Acorns showered off the tree on to the dead leaves below. Big ones, small ones, shiny ones, dull ones, oval and round, fell to the ground. The children gathered them up as fast as they could and it was not long before the sack was half full.

'I think this is enough for today,' said Dick. 'We have a long way to carry the sack, and if it is too heavy we shall never manage it. We'll come back tomorrow for the rest.'

'What will you do?' said Cherry to the Acorn Man. 'Will you come home with us, or do you belong in the forest?'

The Acorn Man took off his round hat, and said:

> 'Who will shelter me,
> Comfort me, love me?
> Only the oak tree,
> Towering above me.'

'Let's make him a house,' said Dick. 'It won't take long because he is so small.'

So the children scooped out a hole between the roots of the oak, and lined it with moss, and made a door-mat of pine needles. The Acorn Man smiled and waved his hat. He crept inside, first wiping his feet on the door-mat.

'How can we thank you for being so kind?' said Cherry. The little man replied:

> 'Put a crumb on my plate,
> And a drop in my cup,
> And merrily, merrily
> I will sup.'

Dick found a last crumb of bread in his pocket and laid it on an oak leaf in the doorway of the house. Cherry found a drop of water on a frond of bracken, and tipped it into the smallest acorn cup she could find.

'Good-bye! Good-bye!' called the children.

'Good-bye!' said the Acorn Man, lifting his little silvery hand to his lips.

Then Dick and Cherry went home, finding the half-filled sack heavy enough, but so proud and excited that they did not mind their arms aching, and their feet slipping in the damp places.

Their father was pleased with the store of acorns and tipped them into the bin. There was room in the bin for many more, and the next morning the children went out again with the sack. They had not spoken about the Acorn Man to their parents. They were not sure how their story would be believed, and they remembered how the Acorn Man had put his hand to his lips as if begging them to keep him a secret.

They made their way quickly to the place where the oak-trees grew. They arranged the sack and began to pick up the acorns left over from the day before. There were not many. While they were working, the Acorn Man came yawning and stretching out of his little house among the roots. He rubbed his eyes, bowed to the oak tree, and said:

> 'Oak tree, oak tree,
> Hear when I call,
> Pitter-patter, pitter-patter,
> Let the acorns fall.'

Once again the acorns fell like rain and the children had only to gather them up. When they ate their dinner, they saved a crumb of bread and cheese for the leaf plate, and squeezed some juice from a late blackberry into the acorn cup. When it was time to go home, the Acorn Man once again put his silvery hand to his lips, so once again they did not tell their father and mother about their new friend.

Each morning, the children took the sack into the forest, and the Acorn Man helped them. Each evening they brought the sack home, heavy with acorns.

One day, when they had almost finished their task, there was a sudden flurry of snow. One minute they were laughing

and talking and rustling among the dead leaves; the next
minute the air was thick with snow, snow in their faces,
snow in their eyes, snow in their mouths, snow melting
down their necks. The world they knew was blotted out.

'Let's go home quickly!' shouted Dick, grasping Cherry
by the hand. 'Once the path is covered we'll never find our
way. Come along!'

T.T.S. – 6

They dragged the sack between them, each holding on and pulling. This kept them together. When they were near the cottage, tired and frightened, their father came to meet them, and their mother, wrapped in her cloak, stood by the open door, peering out.

The children could tell by the way their parents hugged them and kissed them how worried they had been.

After supper, their father made up the fire with logs, and they all drew close.

'We don't need any more acorns,' said their father. 'The bin will be full when I've tipped the last sackful in. You've been good children, working so hard and never complaining.'

'But we liked doing it,' said Cherry.

'Oh yes, perhaps you did, but you must have got weary, searching for the acorns among the fallen leaves. I know, because I've often done it myself.'

'We liked doing it, really and truly,' said Dick.

'And we had the Acorn Man to help us,' added Cherry.

'The Acorn Man!' said their mother. 'Now who was he? I hope you haven't been talking to strangers.'

'He's just a fancy,' said their father. 'Just a childish fancy.'

'No, Father, the Acorn Man was real, not made-up. He could talk,' said Cherry.

'And eat and drink,' said Dick.

'And sing.'

'Like this.' Then they both sang:

> 'Oak tree, oak tree,
> Hear when I call,
> Pitter-patter, pitter-patter,
> Let the acorns fall.'

'We wanted to bring him home, but he asked to live in the forest. Like this:

> 'Who would shelter me,
> Comfort me, love me?
> Only the oak tree
> Towering above me.

'And he begged for just a bite and a sip, like this:

> 'Put a crumb on my plate,
> A drop in my cup,
> And merrily, merrily,
> I will sup.'

The children told the whole story from the beginning when Dick made the little man from the two acorns and the pins he had in his pocket.

'Oh, Dick,' said Cherry, when they had told everything. 'We forgot! We never gave him any supper today.'

'No, we didn't. When the snow came so suddenly, we just picked up the sack and hurried home.'

'And we ought not to have told about him,' Cherry said sadly. 'He always put his little pin hand to his lips when we said good-bye. He meant us to keep him a secret.'

'I'm sure he didn't mean that you were not to tell us,' said their mother. 'He just didn't want curious or unkind people to know about him. I'll knit a pair of red woollen blankets – no bigger than a handkerchief – to keep the little fellow warm at night.'

'That would be a good idea,' said Dick. 'And when the snow is over we'll take them and go back to the oak-tree and see how he is getting on.'

The snow lay thick and white and it was several weeks before the children, wearing their boots and with scarves tied over their heads, were allowed to go as far as the oak trees.

With no sack to hamper them this time, they soon reached the trees, and they knelt down and looked between the roots. The hole was still there, lined with moss, and the door mat of pine needles was in its place. Cherry shook it and put it back.

'The house is empty,' said Dick sadly. 'The Acorn Man has gone.'

Cherry stroked the carpet with her finger.

'But it's warm!' she whispered. 'He can only have gone a minute ago.' She bent down until her face was level

with the moss, to get a clearer view. 'Dick, look! He hasn't gone after all. He's fast asleep.'

Dick looked again. Yes, the Acorn Man was lying deep in the moss, with just bits of his brown shell showing.

Cherry spread the soft red blankets carefully over him, leaving his head uncovered. His little round hat was hanging on the wall on a peg made from a thorn.

'He'll wake next year,' said Cherry.

Dick and she shivered as they stood up and the wind blew in their faces. As they hurried home, the feathery snow began to fall once more.

'Old Mother Goose is shaking her feather bed,' said Cherry.

As they left the oak tree behind and went through the forest, they sang together:

> 'Mother Goose, Mother Goose,
> Shake your feather bed,
> Let the feathers fall,
> Softly on my head.
>
> Let the feathers fall,
> Soft and white and deep,
> But do not wake the Acorn Man,
> Lying fast asleep.'

Through the Window

ONCE upon a time there was a little girl in bed. She opened her eyes and looked out of the window. There was the branch of a tree across one corner of the window. Sometimes it was bare and brown. Sometimes it had green leaves that rustled and quivered. Sometimes it had hard, yellowish pears among the leaves. But this day it had a bird, riding on the tip, see-sawing up and down.

The little girl often saw birds in the garden and in the winter she threw crumbs for them to eat. But this bird was different. He was a thrush and he looked straight in through the window into her eyes as if he knew her. He put his head on one side and nodded. He half-spread his wings and danced a step or two on the branch. Then he sang a song, short and sweet and clear. She could hear every note separately. She could understand what every note meant.

> 'Little curly head
> Sitting up in bed,
> Would you like to be
> A bird like me?'

'Yes, I would indeed,' thought the little girl.
The bird nodded again and sang:

> 'No more talking,
> No more walking,
> Only singing,
> Only winging.'

The bird hopped along the branch until he could reach the window with his beak. He tapped on the pane three times, tap, tap, tap, and sang again:

> 'Little curly head
> Sitting up in bed,
> Would you like to be
> A bird like me?'

'Oh yes, I would!' said the little girl, out loud. 'Indeed I would. I want to be a bird more than anything else in the world!'

She wanted this so badly that her heart changed into the heart of a bird. Her mind changed into the mind of a bird. Her skin changed into feathers and her arms into wings. Her shape changed into a bird's shape and her legs and feet into legs as thin as wire, with curved, spreading toes. She wasn't a girl any longer. She was a bird.

She found she could easily hop out of bed and across the room and out of the open window. Then she perched on the branch to see what else she could do. Her toes gripped the branch securely and she could turn her head from side to side and peck at a speck on the bark. She wondered if she could fly. She flapped her wings up and down, and then, leaving go with her claws, she launched into the air like a ship into the ocean.

She could fly! She could go higher or lower, faster or slower, swerving and glancing, curving and dancing.

She was so happy that she opened her beak and sang for joy. Out of her beak came a waterfall of song, pouring forth like a spring from the rocks, note after note, pure as crystal.

When she was tired of flying and singing, she rested on the grass and looked around. The garden, which had seemed empty, was as crowded as a city square. There were birds everywhere, big and small, dull and gay, alone and in groups. They were all watching her, and each bird was quite different from all the others.

She had always thought of birds as being like each other, starlings like starlings, robins like robins. Now she saw how wrong she had been. The birds were as different from each other as human beings. Some looked kind, some disagreeable; some silly, some wise; some neat and clean, some untidy and dirty. But all were curious. They never took their bright eyes off her and she began to feel shy and awkward. None of them said a word.

Presently she recognized the thrush who had sung to her from the pear tree, and she said timidly:

'I have only been a bird for a little while. You, I know, were hatched out of an egg and have always been a bird. Please help me. There is so much I don't know, so much I have to learn.'

'I will call my mate,' said the thrush. 'She is used to explaining things to the young. She will tell you anything you want to know.'

He whistled to his mate, who flew quickly to his side. She stroked the new bird with her beak and said gently:

'I will do what I can to help you. You shall be my adopted daughter.'

'And we will help you too,' chirped all the other birds, gathering round. They showed her how to preen her wings and smooth her feathers and tuck her head under her wing when she was sleepy.

'At first we were jealous,' said the nightingale. 'I am thought to be the most beautiful singer and I was afraid that you were going to take my place.'

'I, too,' said the kingfisher, flashing by. 'I feared you were going to outshine my bright feathers.'

'I was anxious lest you should soar into the blue of the sky,' said the lark, 'where only I may go, and the eagle who is the king of us all.'

'You need not be afraid,' laughed the new bird. 'I am not beautiful or clever. I only want to be happy and to make friends. What am I like?' she added, turning her head and trying to see herself.

'You must come and look in the pool,' said her adopted mother, fluttering ahead to the pool in the garden, whose water was clear as a mirror. The new bird perched on the edge and leaned over. She saw a small bird with snow

white feathers, deep pink on the head with a yellow crest. Her feet, too, were pink. The bird reminded her of something, but she could not remember what. Perhaps it was of herself in bed the morning before, with her yellow curls and rosy cheeks and white nightgown.

The other birds named her 'Carol' because of her clear voice and she almost forgot she had ever had another name.

The days passed and Carol became more used to being a bird and not a child. She sometimes flew round the house and looked in at the windows, seeing her mother sewing, her father working, her sister and brother playing. But they hardly seemed to belong to her any more. They were like people she had read about in a story book, or met long ago in a dream.

Even her little brother who had been her dearest playmate seemed strange, though the sight of his toys on the nursery floor reminded her of something half-forgotten. But she turned away and spread her wings and flew back into the sunshine. This was her world now, sun and air and tree-top joy.

Carol's new family, the birds, took her on journeys to distant woods where wild fruits grew, and to strange lakes where the flat water-lily leaves were strong enough to land on, like islands. She found new pleasures in walking on the dewy grass at sunrise, and waking in the middle of the night to hear the nightingale singing to the moon. Every day, every hour, there was something fresh to see, or hear, or do.

The older birds, especially her adopted mother, the thrush, often warned her to beware of the bird-catcher.

'He is cunning,' they said. 'He is full of tricks. When you least expect it, you will find yourself in one of his snares.

He has nets as fine as cobwebs, but strong as wire, and once you are entangled in them you can never get free. The more you struggle, the tighter draws the net.'

'I'm not afraid of the bird-catcher,' said Carol. 'He looks a harmless old man with his white beard and spectacles.'

She was so sure of herself that she and some of her lively friends flew round and round him, mocking him and calling:

> 'Bird-catcher, bird-catcher,
> Crafty and sly,
> You'll NEVER get me
> However you try!'

The bird-catcher shook his fist at them and muttered: 'You wait! You just wait!'

One day, Carol was up early to visit the raspberry canes and refresh herself with the freshly ripened fruit. Just as she pecked a perfect berry, something fine but strong tightened over her, pressing her wings to her body and tangling her feet so they could not kick. It was the bird-catcher's net. The bird-catcher himself appeared from behind a bush, took her in his hard brown hands, and carried her away, chuckling: 'Now you are mine, my little angel. Now you are mine, my shining jewel. I must keep you safe, and never let you go.'

The bird-catcher took Carol away and shut her in a small cage with close bars across the front. She could not stretch her wings. She could only raise her crested head and sing. She sang song after song, asking to be set free, homesick for the garden and the freedom of the sky.

The bird-catcher listened to her songs and rubbed his hands joyfully together.

'I shall get a fine price for you,' he said. 'A fine price for such a rare bird with such a sweet voice.'

In the evening, when the bird-catcher was having his supper, Carol's adopted parents, the thrushes, came to see her. They tried to cheer her by telling her the news from the garden.

Carol listened, but would not be comforted.

'Help me to get free,' she begged. 'Only help me to get free.'

On the third evening the thrushes found her even more miserable.

'I think I am to be sold tomorrow,' she said. 'My cage has been specially cleaned out and the wires in front rubbed free from rust. The bird-catcher held me tightly and wiped my feet and legs to make them shine. He has tried to cheer me by bringing me treats, a lump of sugar and a sprig of fresh groundsel. We must say good-bye. I shall never see you again.'

The thrushes stood silent, with drooping heads.

Suddenly the father thrush said:

'I have an idea that might save you. When the bird-catcher opens your cage to give you breakfast, lie down as if you were ill. He will pick you up to find out what is wrong, and may hold you loosely. Then you can struggle with all your might and escape.'

The next morning, Carol did as he had suggested. She lay on the floor of her cage when the bird-catcher opened the door.

'Come! Come!' he said gruffly. 'You mustn't be poorly on the very day I am going to sell you in the bird-market. Let me feel if you are warm.'

He lifted her gently with so loose a grip that she had no

difficulty in suddenly twisting her body, fluttering her wings, and flying beyond his reach.

Carol was careful, now, to keep out of the way of the bird-catcher and she no longer flew round him, mocking him. She had not forgotten the cramped little cage and the touch of his hard hands. But she was not as happy as she had been before. She jumped at every unusual sound, fearing that it was the bird-catcher's footsteps, and shrank from every shadow lest he should be hiding there. If a cobweb brushed her wing, she cried out in terror, imagining that it was his cruel net.

Summer had come, and her adopted mother laid five blue, speckled eggs in a nest lined with mud. She sat on them day and night, thinking only of the little ones which would hatch out when the time came. All the birds in the garden were nest building and laying eggs. Carol, alone, had no wish to make a nest or lay an egg. She grew lonelier and lonelier.

One day, Carol looked in the windows of her old home to see what her family were doing. Her father was polishing his riding boots. Her big sister was sewing silver beads on to a party dress. Her little brother was making a train out of empty boxes. 'Ch-Ch-Ch!' he said, puffing his cheeks out as he pushed the train along.

She wished she were there with him, building a bridge, or working the signals.

Then she looked in the window of her old bedroom and there was her mother, sitting on her little white bed, crying bitterly.

'She is crying for me!' thought Carol. 'She wants me to come home.' As she saw her mother's tears, her bird's heart changed into a human heart. She, too, wanted to go home.

But how could she change her bird's body into a child's body? How could these wings change to arms, these feathers to smooth skin? Would she have to be a bird for ever?

Carol asked the thrush what to do and the thrush looked puzzled.

'I can't help you,' she said. 'I am not very clever. You must ask the grey parrot who lives over the hill. He is very clever indeed. He is a hundred years old and he lives with an old lady who is a hundred years old too. *She* is deaf and nearly blind and very forgetful, but he has sharp ears and keen eyes and never forgets anything. He might be able to help you.'

Carol thanked her and flew off over the hill. She came to a white house with a lawn like green velvet, and on the lawn sat an old lady, in a basket chair. The old lady was fast asleep. Beside her was a grey parrot, sitting on a perch.

'Perch beside me, little bird,' said the parrot. 'I suppose you have come to me for advice. Well, what do you want? Wise though I am, I can't give you good advice if you don't tell me what is wrong. Don't be afraid. Speak up!'

Carol told the grey parrot exactly what she wanted.

'Changing birds into children isn't easy,' he grumbled, putting his head on one side. 'It isn't easy at all, especially as you changed into a bird because you wanted to be a bird. You'll just have to want very, very hard to change back. Perhaps you can get another human being to help. Two lots of wishes are better than one.'

'Thank you,' said Carol, bowing low. 'Thank you, wise grey parrot.'

She flew back to her own garden wondering how she could get another person to help. While she was still wondering, darkness fell and the lights in the house were put out, one by one. She went to the window of the room where her parents lay sleeping and tapped on the pane. She sang:

'I am your daughter,
My arms are wings,
My mouth is a beak
That pecks and sings.
My speech is a song
And feathered my skin.
Pity me! Pity me!
Let me come in!'

Her father only sighed and turned over. Her mother threw out an arm as if to draw someone to her side, but she did not wake.

Then she went to the room where her sister lay sleeping and tapped on the pane. She sang:

'I am your sister,
My arms are wings,
My mouth is a beak
That pecks and sings.
My speech is a song
And feathered my skin.
Pity me! Pity me!
Let me come in!'

But her sister only ran her fingers up and down the sheet as if she were playing the piano, and did not wake.

Then she went to the room where her little brother slept. He was soundly asleep, not moving a finger. She was sure nothing would wake him. She tapped on the pane and sang:

> 'I am your sister,
> My arms are wings,
> My mouth is a beak
> That pecks and sings.
> My speech is a song
> And feathered my skin.
> Pity me! Pity me!
> Let me come in!'

Her little brother leapt out of bed and opened the window and leaned out so far she was afraid he would fall.

'You've come back at last,' he said, stretching out his arms, leaning far over the sill.

'Be careful! Hold tight!' she cried, as his bare feet slipped on the floor. 'Oh, take care!'

But what had happened? She had spoken with a human voice. She was holding him with human hands. She had pushed him back into safety and they were both standing together on the bedroom floor.

'Where have you been?' asked her brother. 'Oh, how I've missed you. I've had no one to play with. When I heard your tap on the window I was dreaming of you and when I heard you singing, I knew you had come home.'

'It was our two wishes that brought me back,' said Carol, 'yours and mine, just as the grey parrot said.'

Then they both got into his warm bed and Carol told her adventures while he said 'Oh!' and 'Ah!' whenever anything exciting happened. She had just reached the end when she found he had dropped asleep and she fell asleep too. So their mother found them in the morning. The little daughter who had vanished through the window had returned home.

Room for a Little One

MINNIE lay dozing and dreaming in front of the kitchen fire. The sun was shining and the birds were singing and it would have been a good day to go into the garden, there was so much going on outside; but Minnie felt too lazy to move. She had had a busy and trying time recently, and now she was going to relax.

Only the day before, Tommy, the last of her last family of kittens, had been given away. Mrs Plum had found a good home for him at a farm near by, and Minnie was sure he would be happy. He had been a particularly difficult kitten to train and had made more fuss than his three sisters put together when it came to being washed, or settling for sleep when it was bedtime. In spite of Minnie's care, he had done considerable damage in Mrs Plum's kitchen. The curtains had loose threads where he had climbed them and got his claws caught in the material. The floor still showed the stain where he had upset Mrs Plum's bottle of cochineal while she was making pink coconut mountains for tea.

It was a blessing that he was going to live on a farm, with

rats and mice to chase, and plenty of space for him to run about freely. Also, thought Minnie severely, there were several other cats on the farm, old and experienced animals who would keep young Tom in his place, and see that he behaved himself.

Minnie was an old and experienced cat herself. She had just had her tenth birthday, and had had more than fifty kittens in her time. Even Mrs Plum had lost track of the exact number, and Minnie herself never managed to count to double figures. Looking back over her long and useful life, her many kittens lost their separate identities. She remembered them just as small, furry, lively, wriggling creatures, always hungry, always wanting something done for them, never content to stay quietly in the box with their mother once they had learned to climb out.

A few outstanding kittens left a clearer memory. There was one who nearly drowned in Mrs Plum's scrubbing pail; another who had been stung by a wasp; another who had swallowed a fish-bone. All had needed endless washing and scolding, and all had needed endless loving and mothering.

'It's nice to be able to lie here just as long as I feel inclined,' thought Minnie. 'If Tom had still been with me I should be jumping up every minute to chase him out of the coal-scuttle, or to hook his ball from under the cupboard. I don't mind if I don't have any more kittens for a long time. I'm getting old and tired.'

Minnie licked her right paw, yawned, rolled over, and dozed off. The kitchen clock ticked, the coals settled in the grate, and she slept as only a mother cat without her kittens can sleep.

Suddenly, while Minnie was dreaming that Tom had climbed the curtains and couldn't get down, the back door was opened and shut with a bang. Mrs Plum was talking anxiously to Mr Hole, the gardener. Minnie knew by the tone of their voices that they were excited and worried.

'Leave it to me!' said Mrs Plum, 'I'll do my best, but Minnie knows her own mind, and it's not easy to persuade her to do what she doesn't want.'

'I hope you'll be successful,' said Mr Hole, 'and I wish I could stay and see how you get on. It's the only hope the little thing has of keeping alive. I'll look in this evening. Good-bye!'

Once again the kitchen door opened and closed.

Minnie lay still, but she was now wide awake. The tip of her tail beat impatiently on the rug, and her eye-lids opened a slit to show a gleam of green.

Mrs Plum was carrying something very carefully in one hand, cuddling it against her blouse, and with the other hand she pulled Minnie's box from the corner of the kitchen, and put it on the hearth-rug. Then she laid the thing she was carrying gently in the box.

The box had been Minnie's bed and her kittens' cradle all her life. When she was younger, it had been kept in the shed, but nowadays it was always in the warm kitchen. Even then she did not often sleep in it when she was by herself. She preferred the cushion on Mrs Plum's chair, or even the little oven where the sticks were put to dry.

'Get into your box, Minnie,' said Mrs Plum in a coaxing voice. 'Get in and see what Mr Hole found in the grass in the paddock.'

Minnie understood quite well what Mrs Plum was saying, but she made no attempt to move. She was too comfortable where she was.

'Come along, Minnie love,' coaxed Mrs Plum. 'I don't

know what to do for the best. You're the only one who can help. Come along, now.'

She picked Minnie up and dropped her gently into the box.

While she was in Mrs Plum's arms, Minnie had been soft and loose as if she hadn't a bone in her body. Once in the box, she stiffened. Her eyes opened wide. The fur along her spine rose slightly. She lashed her tail.

The thing that Mrs Plum had put into the box was both familiar and strange. It was small and brown and furry and seemed very young. But it had a curious smell that did not belong to any kitten Minnie had ever known. The thing was alive, she could see it breathing, and seemed to be terrified. It crouched down in an odd way and looked from side to side with huge dark eyes. But its ears – its enormous, long, narrow ears! It was no member of her family, of that she was certain. She drew back her upper lip and spat under her breath.

Then, her fur still bristling slightly, she sprang out of the box and on to Mrs Plum's chair, and began to wash herself. Was she imagining it, or was there a faint, unusual smell clinging to her?

'Oh, Minnie, Minnie,' cried Mrs Plum. 'Have a heart! Give the little thing some love! It hasn't got a mother and you could be such a good one if you tried.'

Once again she lifted Minnie into the box. Once again Minnie spat quietly and jumped out.

Mrs Plum got on with her work, shaking her head at Minnie as she passed by, and muttering: 'Cruel! Heartless! You ought to be ashamed of yourself.'

Minnie closed her eyes and pretended to be asleep.

But Minnie was far from feeling even drowsy. She was upset and extremely wide awake. The little thing in the box

had a mother somewhere, she was sure, and the mother ought to come and take care of it. Why, in all her long life, she had never *lost* a kitten, though several had been mislaid for a time! Once one had been shut in a cupboard by mistake, and another had fallen asleep in a wardrobe inside a bedroom slipper.

It was enough to bring up her own children in the way they should go, without taking on other people's.

Minnie turned round twice on the soft red cushion and settled herself in her favourite curled-up position, her nose resting on her back feet and her front paws doubled under. But she still felt upset. She listened to the usual sounds of the clock ticking and the fire burning and caught, as well, the rapid, light panting of the stranger. Then, as she listened, she heard a new sound, so faint that only a mother's ear could catch it. The stranger was shivering. In spite of the warm fire and the comfortable cradle lined with blanket, it was shaking with cold or fear, or both.

This time Minnie did not have to think. She did not need

to make up her mind what to do. She simply jumped off the chair, padded quickly across the floor, and got into the box. She lay down and reached out a furry arm and drew the little creature closely to her. Almost at once it stopped shivering and nestled against her as naturally as one of her own children.

Gradually the panting stopped. Minnie purred drowsily, singing the lullaby that she had sung to so many sleepy kittens.

'Well I never,' murmured Mrs Plum, peering into the box. 'My dear, good Minnie! Now, maybe, the little thing will have a chance.'

When Minnie next woke up she knew that it was time to wash her adopted son. She began with his face, made a good job of his long, pointed ears, both inside and outside, and worked her way to his tail. This proved to be a neat, white, furry blob, much easier to manage than the long, whisking tails to which she was accustomed.

When Mrs Plum called her to her supper of fish and milk, she was sorry to see that the new son had been given only a saucer of sliced carrot and a lettuce leaf.

'Just leave it, my dear,' she whispered in one of his long ears. 'There's no nourishment in *that* rubbish. You'll never grow big and strong without fish and milk.' But to her disgust, he nibbled at the lettuce with delight and crunched the carrot, his nose wobbling in a charming way as he ate.

Mrs Plum called the adopted child 'Jack' because of a rhyme she knew which went:

> Jack be nimble
> Jack be quick,
> Jack jump over
> The candlestick.

This Jack hadn't a candlestick within reach, as the pair of shining brass ones were up on the mantelpiece, but he would certainly have jumped over them if he had had a chance. Minnie was amazed at his springing powers. He jumped over the side of the box when he wanted to play on the floor, so different from her kittens, who had had to scramble out as best they could. He crossed the floor in leaps and bounds and when his food was put down for him, he got across the rug in one mighty leap. Minnie gave up worrying over his peculiar diet, which Mrs Plum seemed to understand perfectly.

Minnie did not have to teach Jack to lap milk without paddling in the saucer, or encourage him to eat the potato as well as the liver. He knew exactly how to manage his food. Indeed, he knew so much that she was quite glad there were still one or two things to do for him, such as washing his face and keeping his long ears spotless.

Of course he was naughty sometimes, like all young things, and upset Minnie's milk or got dirty among the coal. All the same, he was much less trouble than any of her kittens had been. He did not try to climb the curtains or the legs of the chairs, and he never attempted to pounce on Mrs Plum's knitting or unwind her ball of wool. He liked to play chasing games, round and round the kitchen and under the furniture, but when Minnie was tired, he went on playing by himself.

They slept together in the box and Minnie grew so used to him that his queerly shaped ears and white bob-tail became quite ordinary.

One fine day, Mrs Plum took her knitting into the garden, and Minnie and Jack came too, to enjoy the sunshine. This was an occasion when her kittens would nearly have driven

Minnie mad, climbing trees and getting stuck, swallowing flies and choking, and mewing furiously whenever a bird flew by. But Jack could look after himself. He leapt all over the lawn and the flower beds, nibbling a leaf here, a flower there, or a blade of grass, and accepting a ripe raspberry from Mrs Plum's fingers. He was looking his best, fur clean and shining, tail like snow, inquisitive nose wobbling with curiosity. Minnie felt full of pride for her adopted son.

Just then she looked up, and saw that they were being closely observed by three of her neighbours, all friends of long standing, and parents of many fine families of kittens. Mrs Dinah was on the top of the wall, Mrs Betsy halfway up the cherry tree, and old Mr Titus on the roof of the summer house. She felt prouder than ever.

'Meet my adopted son, Jack!' she called to them. 'Isn't he a handsome creature?' and as the three friends agreed with approving smiles, Minnie purred with pride and pleasure and Jack leapt over a clump of sweet williams.

Children of the Mist

THERE was once a little island in the sea called the Island of the Tower. This was because there was an old, ruined tower on it, so old that no one knew who had built it, or for what purpose. The people on this island were friendly folk, and happy in their own way, though their life was not eventful or exciting.

There were a few small shops on the island, a church, a school, and a piece of flat ground where the children could play games. A boat came once a week from the mainland, bringing them stores and news of the world beyond.

The children living on the Island of the Tower were as gay and hardy as you could find anywhere. They learned when very young to swim and to manage a rowing boat, and each child had a boat of his own at an age when children on the mainland would be longing for a bicycle or roller skates. They could row with great skill and bring their boats safely on to the shore, tying them up with proper sailors' knots to the iron rings which their fathers had fixed to the rocks.

There were many other islands near by, some only big enough for sea-birds to perch on, and others too bare and rocky for the building of houses. But all were good to play on and the children visited them in turn in the summer-time, playing sometimes on one and sometimes on another.

However wild and rocky the islands were, the children knew of some spot where a boat could be pulled on shore without damage.

If, by mistake, the children played later than they had intended, and dusk was falling, they lit a lantern so that their anxious mothers, watching from the top of the ruined tower, could see a speck of light moving over the dark water, and know that their children were rowing home as fast as they could.

Twin children named Colin and Dolly lived in one of the cottages on the Island of the Tower. They shared a boat between them and together could row it with great speed and ease. If they had a race with other children, they always won, keeping perfect time with their oars.

One hot summer, when the school was closed for the holidays, Colin and Dolly visited the other islands in turn, spending a day on each.

'Tomorrow,' said Colin, after Dolly and he had returned from one of these outings, 'we will go to the Island of the Mist. We've only been there once before, when we were too young to row ourselves.'

'I shouldn't go there,' said their father. 'It is difficult to find a good place to land. The shore is so rocky.'

'Visit one of the others a second time,' suggested their mother. 'The one where the sea-pinks grew, or the one where you found the rainbow shells.'

'It's a dull, dreary spot,' went on their father. 'Nothing to see and nothing to do. Come out fishing with me. I'll try my new nets.'

But the more their parents talked against visiting the island, the more the twins wanted to go.

The next day was sunny, and Colin and Dolly set off early in their boat with a picnic in the knapsack. Their father gave them many warnings not to be late home, and to beware of the mist which gathered quickly and gave the island its name. As they drew near to the island, they saw the sharp rocks sticking up on the beach and Colin rowed slowly while

Dolly looked for a clear place to land. She soon found a narrow inlet edged with sand and they pulled the boat up safely.

There was, as their father had said, nothing interesting on the island. There were no pretty shells and no flowers except prickly sea-holly. There were no trees or bushes, no caves or springs, in fact nothing except rocks and sand dunes and thin, dry grass. The only thing that was rather attractive was a large hollow, flat at the bottom, with low sand hills round it. The floor of the hollow was marked all over with faint prints, blurred by the wind, prints too large for sea birds, too small for people.

It was sheltered in this hollow and a good place in which to eat their picnic, but neither Colin nor Dolly felt comfortable there.

'Let's go back to the beach,' said Dolly.

'And eat our food where we left the boat,' added Colin.

They both felt happier sitting on a rock on the shore, though the wind flapped Dolly's hair in her face and blew the fine sand into their eyes and on to their bread and cheese.

'Well,' said their father, when they were back at home, 'what did you think of the Island of the Mist?'

'It's dull and dreary, just as you said, Father.'

'And we couldn't find anything to do.'

'That's why we're home so early.'

But even after this disappointing visit, Colin, in particular, kept thinking about the strange island. He wished he had stayed longer and explored more thoroughly. He felt he had missed something.

'Father,' he said a week later. 'I think I'll visit the Island of the Mist again.'

'I don't want to come,' said Dolly. 'I'm going to take my

doll to the green and meet the other girls and we're going to have a competition for the prettiest doll.'

'It doesn't matter,' said Colin quickly. 'I'd rather go alone.'

'I can't allow that,' said their father firmly. 'If you must go to that wretched place again, you must take a companion.'

'But Father –' began Colin.

'You heard what I said, Colin. You are not to go alone. I told you before how quickly the mist gathers and before you know where you are, you are lost in a grey, swirling cloud . . .'

Colin soon found four friends willing to go with him, though they all admitted that their parents tried to persuade them to go somewhere else.

'What is the mystery?' asked one boy, as they untied their boats.

'I don't know,' said Colin. 'I suppose it's just that the mist gathers so quickly.'

'I think there are old stories about the island,' said another boy, 'stories of people who landed and were never seen again. I'm surprised that our parents believe such nonsense.'

'So am I.'

The sun shone and the boys whistled and sang as they rowed. They soon reached the island and pulled their boats up the narrow inlet that Colin and Dolly had found before. They had their picnic first and then explored the island carefully. They found nothing of interest and someone suggested playing hide-and-seek as there was nothing else to do.

The boy who was 'he' crouched in the middle of the hollow, his hands over his eyes, and counted a hundred before leaping up and starting his search for his companions. The hiding places were better than they had hoped. There were so many little ups and downs, ridges and furrows, in the dunes that a boy could easily lie hidden if he kept absolutely flat and still.

Suddenly the boy who was 'he' saw that long swirls of mist, like great grey scarves, were floating over the island. He shouted to the others to run for the boats and even before they had reached the inlet, the sky had turned from blue to grey. Instead of being under an immense arch of blue, filled with light and air, the boys felt themselves enclosed under an umbrella of mist that swung and swayed, damp and cold on their faces and legs.

'Are we all here?' called the first boy as they reached the boats. 'Where's Colin?'

'Colin! Colin! Where are you?' the boys shouted. 'Colin! Colin!'

'I'm coming!' came the reply. 'I'll only be a minute. Don't wait. I'll catch you up.'

'He'll do that all right,' said one of the boys, and the others agreed. Colin could row faster than any of them. They pushed off, rowing strongly, and soon broke through the thick, clinging mist into the clearer air beyond. It was some time before someone said: 'Where's Colin?'

They all stopped rowing. There was still mist behind them, hiding the island from which they had come.

'It would be silly to go back, as we might so easily miss him on the way.'

'He knows the islands better than we do. I think he's home already. Let's row on and find out.'

But when the boys landed on the Island of the Tower they found no sign of Colin. They wanted to row back at once, but their parents refused to allow them and Colin's father insisted that they stayed where they were.

'There's trouble enough come upon us,' he said, 'without taking any more risks. Let every boy stay with his mother. I shall go myself to seek my son.'

'And we shall go with you,' said the fathers of the other boys who had been Colin's companions. They set off at once with lanterns, blankets, and food.

Dusk fell, then night came, and the children were sent to bed though they could not sleep. The others wandered from window to window, scanning the sea for a gleam of light, and listening for the splash of an oar.

The men returned next morning, worn out and hopeless. They had found nothing. The Island of the Mist was still swathed in cloud. They had searched every yard, using their lanterns and calling, but they had heard nothing and seen nothing except the scooped out places where the boys had hidden in their game. They had seen many footprints, but these were no help and the marks of their own boots soon over-laid them.

Colin's boat was still drawn up in the inlet.

During the day the mist cleared and the other men, who had not joined in the earlier search, rowed to the Island of the Mist and spent all day looking, parting the thin, dry grass, peering between rocks, examining every inch of the lonely beach. But they found nothing.

'If he is drowned,' said the men, 'his body will be washed up, like as not, or we shall find him when we draw our nets, lying among the silver fish.'

Days passed and there was no sign of Colin, alive or dead. Everyone mourned for him, but none of the children missed him as much as his twin, Dolly. She missed him sleeping in the bed next to hers, sitting next to her at the table, and sharing all her play.

Her father brought the boat back as it seemed impossible that Colin would ever use it again.

One evening, Dolly was sitting on a sheltered rock, beside an old woman who was knitting socks for her grand-children.

'You have lived here longer than anyone else,' said Dolly to the old woman. 'Tell me, do you know any tales about the Island of the Mist? The boys told me that long ago other people disappeared when visiting it.'

'When I was a little girl,' mumbled the old woman, 'I had a friend who disappeared like your brother. She was playing on the island and the mist came down. Her com-panions called her and tried to pull her towards the boats, but they said she was dancing and wouldn't come.'

'Dancing?' repeated Dolly. 'Dancing? Was she dancing alone?'

'Her friends said she was dancing with other children made of mist, swirling and whirling and waving grey scarves. Then the mist disappeared and the girl had vanished too. Before I was born, there were three children of one family who disappeared in the same way, so I've heard say. The Children of the Mist made them join their dance, and their parents never saw them again.'

Dolly asked the old woman many questions, but she had nothing more to tell. The lost children had gone with the Children of the Mist, she didn't know where or how or why. Her head began to nod over her knitting and Dolly gave up worrying her.

Now Dolly felt sure that Colin was with the Children of the Mist and she planned to go secretly and rescue him. She would go to the island when the mist had blown up, and try to catch a glimpse of him.

Meanwhile, Dolly's parents would not let her land on the island; but she often rowed her boat as near as she dared, and she learned the way so well that she could almost have rowed there blindfold.

Every evening Dolly lay awake till after midnight, looking out of her window and watching the brilliant stars and their shepherdess, the moon. Then, one night, the stars were dim and pale and she saw that a light mist was creeping over the sea. Now was her chance.

She dressed in warm clothes, tiptoed out of the cottage and ran barefoot to the place where her boat was tied to the iron ring. She loosened the rope and rowed quickly in the direction of the Island of the Mist. She could see only a little distance, but she had rowed there so often that she found the way easily and even landed in the right narrow inlet among the rocks.

Dolly ran to the low sand hills surrounding the hollow and lay there without moving, just waiting. Sea-holly pricked her legs but she did not feel the pain. The mist swirled by, cold and clammy, and her hair was drenched

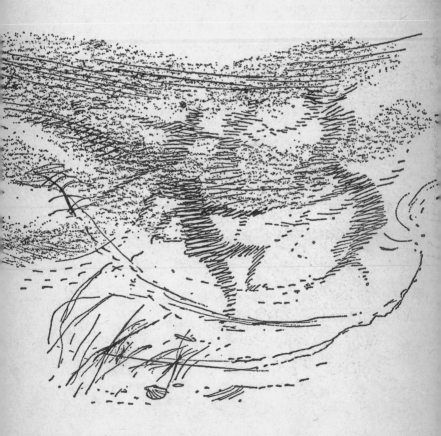

with moisture. Her jersey clung to her wetly. She noticed a grasshopper crouched, like herself, in the sand between two blades of grass. She moved her hand so as not to hurt him.

After a time the mist seemed to be taking on shapes, like trees or bushes with tossing branches. No, they were like people with waving arms and long legs leaping and prancing. They *were* people, she was sure. Her eyes grew used to the dim light and she saw that the hollow was filled with shadowy grey children, dancing in a ring and trailing misty scarves from their outstretched arms.

She looked eagerly from one dancer to another. All were equally grey and shadowy. Then, suddenly, she saw Colin. He was dancing with the others and two of the Children of the Mist were holding his hands, one on either side. But how different he looked from his companions! Their lips were silver — his were red. Their cheeks were white — his were pink. Their hair streamed behind them like smoke — his dark curls clung to his head.

Dolly dared not call his name as she was afraid the dancers would vanish, taking Colin with them. While she was wondering what to do, she felt the grasshopper touching her hand with his feelers. He was shaking his tiny tambourine very gently, and whispering some words. She bent her head as near to him as she could and thought she heard him saying:

> 'A drop of your blood,
> If you love him well,
> Will set him free
> And break the spell.'

Then, with a leap, the grasshopper landed by her ear and whispered the words a second time, shaking his tiny tambourine gently:

> 'A drop of your blood,
> If you love him well,
> Will set him free
> And break the spell.'

A drop of blood was not difficult to give. The prickly leaves of the sea-holly had made many scratches on her legs and drops of blood were oozing from them. She wriggled as near to the dancers as she dared, waited till Colin drew level, and jumped up with a smear of blood on her finger. She just managed to touch his cheek before the other dancers whirled him away. As her finger touched him, the dance stopped and a thin wail went up from the dancers, like the high notes of a violin. They leapt into the air and vanished, leaving the sandy hollow empty in the moonlight, except for Dolly and Colin.

Colin looked puzzled and dazed, as if he had been wakened from a deep sleep, and Dolly had to pull him over the dunes towards the boat. Once he had the oars in his hands, he came to himself and rowed strongly. They sped over the water and were soon back on their own island and Colin tied the boat up with the safe sailor's knot his father had taught him.

'Mother! Father!' cried Dolly. 'Colin is home!' Soon their cottage and all the neighbouring cottages had lights in the windows and were full of laughter and welcome. Everyone asked Colin where he had been and what he had been doing, but his stay with the Children of the Mist was like a dream, forgotten on waking. He could only say they were kind to him and kissed him with cold, silver lips and stroked him with cold, thin hands.

After this, the children living on the Island of the Tower

never again wanted to visit the Island of the Mist. Even when they rowed to the other islands for a picnic or a day's play, they came home before dusk fell and had no need to light their lanterns to reassure their watching, waiting mothers.

After the Tenth Tale

WHILE Shellover the Tortoise was telling the last story, *The Children of the Mist*, the pets noticed that he often yawned and blinked his eyes. Once or twice his voice had grown slow and hesitating, and they thought he might have forgotten what came next, but after a little pause he had gone on till he reached the end.

'If I'd been with Colin,' said the Dog, 'I would never have left his side. I would have chased those Children of the Mist away.'

'I never approve of water,' said the Cat. 'I don't know why they wanted to go out in a boat in the first place.'

'It must be nice to have travelled like Tortoise,' said the Cow. 'I should like to visit strange lands, if Mrs Candy and the rest of you came too.'

'What is your next story called, Tortoise?' asked the Hens from their comfortable perch on the Cow's back.

'I really don't know,' said Shellover the Tortoise, his small mouth opening in a yawn that showed his pink tongue. 'It's time I went to sleep. Tomorrow I shall look for a suitable place where I can dig a hole for the winter.'

'Does that mean there'll be no more stories till the spring?' asked the Cat.

'I'm afraid so,' said Tortoise, yawning again.

'Never mind,' said Mrs Candy, stroking Tortoise's nose gently. 'You've told us so many lovely stories –'

'Ten,' said the Hens, who were always counting something, eggs or chicks or whatever came their way.

'Yes, ten lovely stories, and now you need a rest. We can tell the stories again to ourselves in the winter.'

'I'll tell a Cat one,' said the Cat. 'I remember every word.'

'And we'll tell the Bird one,' said the Hens.

'And I'll tell the *Ugsome Thing*,' said the Dog, who liked that one best.

'Perhaps we can make up a new story to tell Tortoise when he wakes up,' suggested Mrs Candy.

The next day Shellover the Tortoise sleepily explored the garden and chose a spot under a laurel bush where the soil was soft. Helped by the animals, he dug a suitable hole and crept inside. The Dog covered over the last square of his shell which was still showing.

'Good-night, Tortoise,' they said. 'Good-night and sleep well.'

About the Author

Ruth Ainsworth has been writing stories and poems for over thirty years, starting when she was a school girl and a student. She is married and has three sons, now grown up. When they were small and living in the country, she used to tell them endless stories on walks, and *they* told *her* wonderful stories too.

She says she was a natural scribbler, and having her own children around added an inexhaustible fund of riches. She now lives in a village in the Tyne valley, likes reading and walking, and seeing her grandchildren.

Some recent additions to the Young Puffin list

A BROTHER FOR THE ORPHELINES
Natalie Savage Carlson

Sequel to *The Happy Orpheline*. Josine, the smallest of all the orphans, finds a baby left on the doorstep. But he is a *boy*. So the orphans plot and worry to find a way to keep him.

MY FIRST BIG STORY BOOK
ed. Richard Bamberger

A wonderful hoard of nursery rhymes and bedtime stories, ranging from traditional English favourites to strange new tales from other lands.

ROBIN
Catherine Storr

Robin was the youngest of three, and hated it. And then he discovered the shell called the Freedom of the Seas – and became the wonder of his family.

THIS LITTLE PUFFIN ...
compiled by Elizabeth Matterson

A treasury of nursery games, finger plays and action songs, collected with the aid of nursery school teachers all over the British Isles. For parents of under-fives. (*Original*)

THE SECRET SHOEMAKERS
James Reeves

A dozen of Grimm's least-known fairy tales retold with all a poet's magic, and illustrated sympathetically by Edward Ardizzone.

POLLY AND THE WOLF AGAIN
Catherine Storr

In spite of all Polly's cleverness the wolf doesn't give up. But he is as stupid as ever and even little sister Lucy manages to get the better of him.

THE YOUNG PUFFIN BOOK OF VERSE
Barbara Ireson

A deluge of poems about such fascinating subjects as birds and balloons, mice and moonshine, farmers and frogs, pigeons and pirates, especially chosen to please young people of four to eight. (*Original*)

NEW ADVENTURES OF GALLDORA
Modwena Sedgwick

Galldora, the rag doll, has more hair-raising adventures, in this book she saves Marybell and her father from drowning, and hides a top-secret document from thieves after her first trip in an aeroplane. Strangest of all, she saves the day when she is baked in a rabbit pie!

TALES FROM THE END COTTAGE
Eileen Bell

Two tabby cats and a peke live with Mrs Apple in a Northamptonshire cottage. They quarrel, have adventures and entertain dangerous strangers. A new author with a special talent for writing about animals. For reading aloud to 5 and over, private reading 7 plus. (*Original*)

MORE ABOUT TEDDY ROBINSON
Joan G. Robinson

New advenures for the comfortable teddy bear and his friend Deborah. Perfect bedtime reading for four-year-olds.

GEORGE
Agnes Sligh Turnbull

George was good at arithmetic, and housekeeping, and at keeping children happy and well behaved. The pity of it was that he was a rabbit so Mr Weaver didn't believe in him. Splendid for six-years-old and over.